I0545377

FINDING THE UPSIDE OF DOWN

DIONIE MCNAIR

Dedication

To all the victims of bullying I know there are many of you out there silently suffering, afraid to speak out. I understand your pain because I was bullied too.

There is no easy answer. Bullying is endemic in our society. Yet many still do not take it seriously, do not understand the deep, sustained damage perpetrated, verbal, physical, social or cyber, in the home, school or work.

Demand it be stamped out, wherever and however it exists. Do not stay silent, ask for help. Refuse to retreat into a dark place, suicide is not the answer.

Those who love you will light the darkness and help you fight the unrelenting pain that gnaws at you. Never accept a bully's assessment of who you are for their opinion only reflects their own weaknesses and damaged spirit. For you are unique, wonderful and blessed with many talents.

Dig deep, find your individual way to shine, for when you shine with your own bright light, you will believe in yourself. Become too strong to be crushed by the empty words of a bully.

I hope Tabitha's story, *Finding the Upside of Down*, offers a ray of hope to victims, encourages them to tell and talk and to search within themselves for their own unique talent. It doesn't matter what that talent is—volunteering for the SES or CFS, painting, writing a book, saving the whales, running in a marathon, you must find it, foster it and learn to believe in yourself. Only then can a bully's words and actions be stripped of the power to scar your soul.

Books by Dionie McNair

The Abrasaxon's Daughter

The Scorpion's Heart

Single Titles

Finding the Upside of Down

Finding the Upside of Down

ISBN # 978-1-78651-364-9

©Copyright Dionie McNair 2016

Cover Art by Posh Gosh ©Copyright 2016

Interior text design by Claire Siemaszkiewicz

Finch Books

Chapter One

The rough, solid shove against Tabitha's right shoulder demolished her precarious balance as she negotiated the last step. Her pile of textbooks, pencils and new tablet flew from her folded arms and splattered in an arc on the narrow landing. She reached out to save herself but her hand slipped from the rail and she crashed onto her knees with a bone-jarring thud.

"Oops, Tubby Tabby's done a bellyflop, but then, you always were clumsy, weren't you? Such a shame, on your first day at college and all, to make such a scene."

Tabitha flinched at the scathing words, the scorching heat of embarrassment burning across her face as she looked up into Amelia Eckerton's sneering expression. What the hell was she doing here? Why wasn't she at university?

As usual, Tabitha struggled to respond to Amelia taunts, to find the words to refute her cruelty and the courage to say them out loud. As she cowered on her knees, the other students pushed past, stepping nonchalantly over her belongings or shoving them aside so they didn't have to step on them. By the time Tabitha had gathered her composure, Amelia had disappeared down the next flight of stairs. Her knees hurt, her wrist throbbed where she had used it to break her fall and tears of embarrassment burned at the backs of her eyes. As she tried to scramble to her feet with as much dignity as possible, a hand provided support under her elbow.

"You all right?"

Upright once more, Tabitha turned and found a dainty blonde girl by her side.

"I think so. Thank you for helping me," she said.

"I'm Jaclyn," the blonde girl announced as she bent down and began to gather Tabitha's books from the floor. "Here you go," she said as she handed over Tabitha's things. "Good luck. I might see you round."

"Thanks again," Tabitha said loudly as she watched Jaclyn skip down the stairs and disappear in the milling students.

Tabitha's positivity and mettle for her venture into campus life vanished with the helpful stranger. One cruel action of a ruthless bully had shattered her new start and brought the past rushing back with stark cruelty. The throb from her knees underpinned the tremble of shock and dismay as she clutched the handrail to steady herself. Was this year about to be a repeat of Year Twelve, where she had crumbled under the barrage of abuse from Amelia and failed to deliver the work to achieve a satisfactory score for university? Resentment flared and Tabitha stiffened her spine. *No, I will not lose this too. I will not let her get to me.* She consolidated her pile of books, pushed away from the handrail and made her way down the stairs.

Shock rattled through her as she struggled to regain her earlier orientation and negotiate the maze of corridors, but at last, with a sigh of relief, she slipped through the door of room two-one-nine into the half-filled classroom. With surreptitious glances, she studied her companions — a couple of girls huddled in the back corner whispered to each other, and three guys her age sat silently waiting for the lecture to start. One of them looked up as she reached a spare desk.

"Hey, Tabitha Cockell, long time no see," he said.

She looked directly at him, stunned by a flash of recognition. "My God, Alex, what are you doing here?"

"I bombed out in my second year of my vet course, didn't work hard enough. I have to get some money together to go back so took a job at the racing stables," he said. "Boss wants me to have some qualifications so he sent me here."

"Wow," Tabitha exclaimed, stunned at Alex's failure to

6

make the grade at university.

"So where ya been, Tabitha?" Alex asked. "You haven't come on any of the car club cruises with your dad, and you deactivated your Facebook ages ago."

"Yeah. Would love to have been with Dad, because he even lets me drive the car sometimes, but study and work called, and as for Facebook, I stopped using it because there was too much nastiness and shit going on."

"Yeah, it can be like that. Anyway, Tabitha, it's good to see you again. Maybe we should get together to study sometime," Alex suggested.

She nodded. "That would be good, Alex."

As Alex turned to answer a question about textbooks from one of the other students, Tabitha found a seat and prepared to begin. While she waited she glanced surreptitiously at Alex several times. She had always had a thing for him since meeting him four years ago at one of the cruises, but both fathers had made it clear Alex was too old for her.

The door opened and shut as another person arrived. Footsteps came closer. Someone leaned over her shoulder and whispered in her ear.

"Oh my goodness, fancy that, Tubby Tabby — we're in the same class. This is good. We can get reacquainted."

Tabitha cringed as the words cut into her soul. She struggled to hold back the burn of acid bile in her throat as her stomach contracted into a tight ball of grabbing pain. With a sense of foreboding, she glanced up at Amelia — her nemesis — then dropped her gaze back to her books. She had nothing to say.

"Did you have a good trip on the stairs, Tubby?" Amelia chuckled. "And I thought college was going to be so boring, with no one to stir."

"You could've really hurt me, Amelia. Just go away, this isn't high school and we aren't kids anymore," Tabitha muttered, keeping her eyes on her desk.

"Well, well, well, think you're too good for me now, do you? Perhaps I'll have to rectify that before you leave today,

Tubby," Amelia sneered.

"My name is Tabitha. Don't call me that childish name," Tabitha snapped, all her frustration and consternation at Amelia's continuing ridicule adding sharpness to her tone.

"Awww, Tubby, don't be like that," Amelia admonished as she drifted to the back of the room and found a seat.

Tabitha sat stock-still, her hands clenched on the table in front of her, fighting to control the tremble. Her stomach threatened to rebel and she swallowed hard to keep it under control. Of all the people to be in her class. She wanted to run from the room and never come back, but something held her in place—a desire to complete the vet nursing certificate and get a full-time job at the local vet clinic where she now worked part-time.

As she had walked away from her high school graduation, she'd dared to believe the misery of Amelia was behind her. Thirteen years of bullying and angst that had almost destroyed her life. *Well, there's no way she's going to take this from me. I will not buckle.* She would suffer, and struggle with the abuse as she had before, but somehow she would survive this.

Amelia quickly sat down when the lecturer entered the room. He introduced himself as Kayne Smith and invited them to use his given name because they were all adults and he preferred to keep it informal. Apart from the inevitable class member introductions, Tabitha didn't have to say anything and she breathed a sigh of relief when her turn had passed. She found the lecture informative, and thought the first assignment looked challenging but interesting and decided on the spot she would base the report on the vet clinic where she worked, if the manager would give permission.

With a two-hour break between classes, Tabitha walked across to the nearest shopping center, planning to hide in the crowds of shoppers and office workers eating lunch— somewhere Amelia couldn't find her. As she munched on her sandwiches in a corner of the food court, she examined her options. There weren't many—she either put up with Amelia, or she pulled out. She was determined to complete her course. The other thing she decided was not to tell her parents this time. They had been upset and frustrated with the ongoing bullying in school, always jollying her along or offering solutions that failed to work. She was an adult now, so she had to cope with this on her own.

At two when she returned to the college, Amelia, flanked by the other two girls from class, was waiting for her at the end of the corridor.

"So where'd you get to, Tubby Tabby? I missed the fishy smell that emanates from you, Fishbait. I thought we could have lunch together. Mighty antisocial, aren't we?"

"I had a job to do," Tabitha muttered defensively, not willing to admit she had run away to avoid Amelia.

"Never mind, there's always Thursday," Amelia replied.

"Whatever," Tabitha muttered as she pushed past them into the room.

As she took her seat, Amelia leaned over her shoulder. "There's no escape, Fishbait."

Tabitha stared straight ahead at the whiteboard as she tried to ignore the threat that seared her soul. There were always online courses, she thought, but that would mean trips interstate for the contact sections—more fees and more costs. It wasn't an option.

She settled down in her seat, determined not to let Amelia's taunts get to her like they had in Year Twelve, but all through the lecture, she was on edge, all too aware of Amelia behind her, just waiting for a chance to pounce at the end of class.

Tabitha dawdled with her packing up, hoping Amelia would have gone, but she and the girl called Petra who sat next to her in class were waiting in the corridor when she emerged from the classroom.

"So, Tubby, have a good day?" Amelia asked.

"Fine, thank you."

Amelia smirked. "Didn't find it all too hard, did we? I

know you're not the brightest light globe in the box. How you even got in, I don't know. Maybe your mum put in a good word for you. She's pretty good at that, isn't she?"

Tabitha looked directly at Amelia, struggling to make sense of her comments. "What has my mum got to do with it? I got in the same way you did, Amelia—by getting the right score."

"Yeah, like you still got to be a fairy in the ballet concert. Your mum always goes in to bat for you, doesn't she? Either that or you've cheated—too fat to be a fairy, and too stupid to make the grade. Cockles belong in the sea, Fishbait, not stinking up our college," Amelia sneered loudly and gave Tabitha a little shove toward the stairs.

"For goodness' sake, Amelia, we were five, and it wasn't my fault the teacher made you be a tree just because you were too tall to be a fairy."

Amelia pushed her again, harder this time. "But you got to be a fairy, even though Mrs. Edwards said you were too fat. And she was right. You were too fat. You *are* too fat."

"Hey, you. Let up on her, okay? This is college, not the schoolyard you just came from," Alex yelled from the doorway of the classroom.

"What's it to you?" Amelia taunted.

"She's my friend," Alex replied.

"Really?" Amelia exclaimed. "Well, Tabby doesn't need your protection. We go way back, to preschool, in fact. She knows I'm only stirring her." Amelia glared at Alex.

"Well, it looks to me like it's stirring she could do without," Alex replied.

Amelia turned her focus back to Tabitha. "Oh, Fishbait, it looks like you have a friend. Maybe more than a friend, which would be a first, wouldn't it?"

"Shut up, Amelia," Tabitha retorted, totally mortified for Alex. She glanced over to see how he had taken Amelia's suggestive insults and tried to give a small smile in his direction that said sorry. Then she turned to walk down the stairs.

"Oops, looks like I hit a nerve," Amelia mocked.

Tabitha kept walking down the stairs, cloaked in embarrassment, for Alex and for herself. She found it difficult to acknowledge him when he caught up to her. Finally, she summoned up the courage and the voice to speak. "Thank you for helping. I'm sorry about what she said."

"Try not to let it get to you, kid. She's just an immature bitch, that one. The novelty will wear off in a couple of weeks."

"I wish, Alex. She's been bullying me since we were five."

"What a bummer," Alex muttered, a grim expression transforming his face.

"Yeah, I thought I'd seen the last of her at the end of Year Twelve, but here she is, turning up like a bad penny to make my life unbearable again."

"Just ignore her, Tabitha. Anyway, see you Thursday."

"Okay," Tabitha replied and headed to the bus stop. The last thing she wanted to think about was her next day at college, but that was all she did on the long ride home — the next dreaded meeting with Amelia and what she should tell her mother about her first day at college.

As she walked in the door, her mother pounced on her.

"Tell me, young lady," she demanded.

"It's great, Mum. Alex from the car club is in my class. We've already got an assignment too," she informed her mum, trying to sound enthusiastic, but her words came out flat and dull.

"You don't sound all that sure, dear."

Tabitha tried to smile but instead started to cry. "It was good, Mum, but Amelia turned up in my class. I wish she hadn't."

She wiped the tears away and blew her nose with the tissue her mother handed her.

"I hope she's not going to start up all that rubbish from school again. I mean, you're adults now. I thought you said she would be going to university, becoming a doctor or

11

something," her mother said.

A dying sob squeezed her chest with a painful jerk as Tabitha shook her head. She didn't have an answer to her mother's question, but she muttered, "I don't know, Mum. Maybe she didn't get a high enough score."

"Never mind, love. You go and get freshened up. I'm sure it will be fine," her mother reassured her.

Tabitha trailed to her room, the weight of her dilemma heavy on her shoulders and burrowing into her heart. She already knew it was not going to be fine. And she had no other options. Her parents weren't well-off, and they'd already paid her fees. They couldn't afford to lose that money, or pay fees to go interstate to do her course at another college.

By the time she got out of the shower, a bitter anger had invaded her — anger that one person was so determined to destroy her opportunities. Strip her of choices in life. Damn Amelia Eckerton. How dare she be so cruel?

She'd heard her father arrive home some time ago, but she was reluctant to go downstairs and participate in the expected rehash of the day she wanted to forget — she didn't want to see the worry on her parents' faces, as she had last year when she'd struggled to cope with Amelia's bullying. It made her feel sick that she'd caused most of their worry. They were good parents. They had always wanted the best for her, and they didn't deserve this hassle with their only child.

With slow steps, she finally joined them in the dining room. Her mum, of course, had cooked her favorite dinner, ravioli with thick bolognese sauce. For her mum, food was the great healer, the timeless expression of love. Tabitha knew this, accepted this, but felt a deep-seated pain because all that 'love' had made her chubby.

Her dad smiled at her, but she saw the worry under that smile, and guilt swirled in her gut because she'd caused it. She would have to pretend it was all good.

"Mmm, this looks great, Mum," she said, picking up her

fork.

"You all right, honey?" her dad asked.

She looked up at her father and smiled. "I'm fine, Dad."

"Do you think that nasty piece of work will give you more trouble?" he asked.

Tabitha shook her head. "Nah, Dad, I'm sure she's over it by now."

"One would hope so, you're not children anymore," he said and began to eat.

Tabitha's thoughts whirled in her head. No matter what she'd said, Amelia definitely wasn't over it, but it was time to change the subject.

"And you'll never guess, Dad, who turned up in my class. Alex. Apparently he bombed out of vet school."

"That's not good, because that boy has brains."

"He said he might go back, but for now he's working at the stables."

"Well, I hope he does. I'm sure his parents have made sacrifices for him to study."

She knew her father wasn't having a dig, but guilt niggled at her anyway.

* * * *

Thursday came around all too soon, and from the moment she opened her eyes, Tabitha felt tightness grab at her chest and the uneasy slop of her stomach. It got worse with each bus stop on the way, but she refused to give into her body's desire for flight. Today she would have to fight her demons. She made a silent pact with herself, that she would look Amelia in the eyes and tell her to bugger off. Tabitha imagined herself saying it, but immediately felt anxious and tense. It was one thing to intend to do it, to plan to do it, and entirely another to actually do it to Amelia's face.

Tabitha was one of the last to arrive in the classroom. Amelia lounged in the back row with her new friends. Leo, Alex's new mate from the first day, smiled her way as she entered. She smiled back, feeling strengthened by the thought of having at least one friendly face in the room. She swallowed hard on her dry throat, took her pencils out, set up her tablet and switched off her phone, trying to appear competent and calm to anyone watching. But already on edge, she cringed inwardly when someone walked up behind her. Almost unconsciously she mentally curled in on herself, preparing for the taunts. But before they could be thrust at her, the lecturer walked in.

"Amelia, did you need to see me?" he asked.

"No," Amelia muttered, immediately retreating toward the back of the room.

"Then I suggest you find a seat. We've heaps to get through today."

Tabitha heaved a sigh of relief. *Whew, saved by the bell – or the lecturer, actually.*

Then Alex arrived, looking scruffy in what were obviously his work clothes. "Sorry I'm late, got held up at work," he said to Kayne as he wound his way through the desks to his usual seat. He tapped Tabitha on the shoulder as he slipped behind her chair. She grinned up at him then watched him until he was seated. He was such a hunk.

Silence blanketed the room and Kayne began.

The subject matter was fascinating. Tabitha became so enthralled she almost forgot her nemesis lurking at the rear of the classroom. She loved animals with a passion. She had always dreamed of becoming a vet, but her obvious lack of academic ability had soon squashed that idea. She'd mourned her failure to be brainy enough for quite a while, but then decided a veterinary nurse qualification was well within her reach, and would satisfy her love of animals. She already worked one day a week at the local veterinary surgery—cleaning cages, comforting animals and refilling shelves. The clinic manager had promised her another day when she qualified, and perhaps a full-time position in the near future. In the meantime, she had her job Thursday night and every second Sunday afternoon at Mrs. Waldrop's, a quaint little gift shop where you would be guaranteed to find that elusive gift for the person who had everything. Ivy Waldrop could be a formidable lady, with high expectations, but she had a heart of gold and had always treated Tabitha with kindness since she started working in the shop just before Christmas. The only problem was that the college campus was completely in the opposite direction and she had two buses to catch tonight to reach Mrs. Waldrop's, and she wouldn't dare be late.

* * * *

With only fifteen minutes left of class, Tabitha's uneasiness returned. As the lecturer rattled on, right down to the last five minutes, she was almost tempted to ask to leave early, worried she would get caught up by Amelia and miss her bus. She had already packed everything into her backpack as the lecturer outlined the assignment. This needed to be completed in the next fortnight. It sounded interesting, but Tabitha couldn't concentrate on it with Amelia about to scuttle out of the door in readiness to attack her. As they were dismissed, she snatched up her bag and bolted for the door, but Amelia and her friends had already slipped out into the passage.

"You look harassed, Tabitha. You gotta be somewhere?" Alex asked as he came up behind her at the door.

"Yes, I have two buses to catch to get to my part-time job," she told him. "Time is cut fairly fine, and I'm afraid Amelia will hold me up."

"Come on. I'll play bodyguard," Alex said and grinned down at her.

"Really?

Alex laughed then. "Don't be so surprised, Tabitha. I have a younger sister, and she was bullied by a couple of kids in primary school. I really wanted to punch them in their noses, but Dad said no. Caitlin took up karate the next year and gained so much confidence knowing she could take

15

them down if she chose they stopped hassling her."

Tabitha was grateful for Alex's company when, as expected, Amelia was waiting for her. But at the same time, embarrassment washed over her for Alex, who obviously felt obliged to help her. That quickly turned to mortification when Amelia started a sleazy verbal tirade directed at her, about him. Alex glared at Amelia but stayed silent, just putting his hand on Tabitha's back to urge her forward. Tabitha lowered her gaze and hurried down the stairs, and Alex stood with her until the bus arrived, not commenting on the abuse. She made it to work with minutes to spare and knew if there were the slightest delay in the future, she would be late.

* * * *

The following Tuesday she drummed up the courage to ask Kayne if she could leave class ten minutes early on Thursdays, to catch the earlier bus. He understood, but warned if she missed anything or showed signs of failing, he would have to rescind his approval. Tabitha nodded, happy with the outcome as she went off to lunch.

She had just gotten settled back at her desk after the lunch break when Amelia waltzed into the room and, grinning wolfishly, veered so close to Tabitha's desk that her bulky backpack swiped everything on the desk onto the floor.

Amelia paused for just a moment as the clatter echoed around the room. "Oops, so clumsy of me," she muttered in a singsong voice before flicking her long hair over her shoulder and walking away.

Tabitha watched her take her place in the last row of desks before she slipped off her chair to gather up her scattered belongings. Her face blazed with humiliation under the curious scrutiny of the others and the quiet snickering coming from the back of the room. Alex wasn't there yet and no one else offered to help. She was still flustered and unsettled when Alex hurried through the door just in time

16

for the beginning of the lecture, and found it difficult to concentrate. By the end of the class, she felt totally confused about zoonotic diseases and ever so slightly panicky.

Alex came up behind her as she left the classroom. "So did that all make sense to you, Tabitha?"

She shook her head. "No. I'm having trouble concentrating today," she replied, but refrained from telling him that she had been unsettled by Amelia's little stunt. It was extremely embarrassing that she still couldn't cope with Amelia's teasing even though she was now an adult.

"Tell you what, why don't I come over on Saturday and we can go over it together. I have track work at the stables in the morning, but I could be at your place by two."

Overcome by pleasure, excitement and gratefulness, Tabitha grinned. She liked Alex, and his offer to share study was a great idea. "That would be great, Alex. Maybe we could talk about the assignment too. I have some ideas and some notes."

"Great, Tabitha. See you Thursday."

All the way home, Tabitha felt warm inside, and for a while it helped to ease the anxiety about Amelia.

No one was home when she got there and she went straight to her room to review the day's lecture. Instead she found herself doodling Alex's name across her lecture pad, and when she finally went to bed, she was no closer to understanding the contents of the lecture.

Tabitha lay awake and pondered why Amelia hated her so much. Surely it wasn't just the debacle at the ballet concert thirteen years before. It had to be something else, but although Tabitha racked her brains, she couldn't come up with one thing Amelia might hold against her. She planned out imaginary scenarios on how she could act the next time Amelia picked on her, but deep down she knew she would never have the courage to carry any of them through. The only time she had found the courage to fight back and used some of the strategies the counselor had given her, Amelia had called her a cheeky bitch and given her a physical beating, leaving her with a black eye and bruised ribs.

Chapter Two

Tuesday's lectures were always the hardest, because Amelia niggled at her on the way into class and was always waiting afterward. Tabitha had come to rely on Alex's company walking to the bus each week.

When Alex didn't turn up for class Tuesday morning just before mid semester break, she wondered where he was and fully expected a hard time from Amelia on the way home.

At the lunch break, she paused by Leo's desk. "Hey, Leo, where's Alex?"

Leo shook his head. "Dunno. Tried calling him. No answer."

Amelia snickered as she pushed past Tabitha. "Awww, Alex has gone AWOL."

Heat rushed up Tabitha's face and she gave an embarrassed little smile to Leo.

"Just ignore her, Tabitha. I'll let you know if I hear anything."

She nodded and hurried out of the room, planning to meet Jaclyn for lunch. She made her way to the café, all the time aware of Amelia and her two sidekicks shadowing her at a distance. She saw Jaclyn immediately as she entered and waved as she made her way to the table.

"I see you have friends," Jaclyn commented with a touch of sarcasm in her tone.

Tabitha looked over her shoulder. "Yes, I know," she said.

Jaclyn glared at the three girls and Amelia immediately veered away and took a table on the other side of the room.

"Just ignore them, Tabitha," Jaclyn advised.

Tabitha nodded, knowing full well that was not the solution.

Once they'd gotten their food, Jaclyn and Tabitha became absorbed in their conversation, and the tension of Amelia's presence faded.

"So how's the course going?" Jaclyn asked.

"Great. We have our first assignment already and I think I'll do it on work."

"Good idea. I'm not so sure about my course. I thought I would like it because I'm an organized person, but I hate doing Excel."

Tabitha shuddered. "Glad it's not me. I'll stick to animal poop and fluffy kittens," she said.

"So what do you like besides fluffy kittens? Do you like that new girl, Layla? The one who sings *By the Water* and *Thunder on the Beach*?

"I do. I thought about going to her concert later in the year, but have to save up for it or dip into my car savings. The tickets will probably be around a hundred dollars."

"Well, if you decide to go, I'll come with you, although I'll probably need to put the new doll I want for my collection on layby or like you, raid the car savings, if I do." Jaclyn grimaced. "Can't wait to start full-time work—more money."

"Yeah, I already work two jobs to make ends meet. So how long have you been collecting dolls? I collect teddies."

"Wow. So do you want to send me a friend request on Facebook?"

Tabitha shook her head. "I'm not on Facebook anymore because of her," she said, pointing discreetly toward Amelia.

"Oh, bugga. I didn't realize it was that bad."

Tabitha nodded. "It's been bad for a long time."

Jaclyn shuddered. "I don't know how you cope, Tabitha."

Tabitha shrugged. "I just do."

Jaclyn stood up and gathered her things. "Well, better get back to it, at least it's booking travel and accommodation

20

this afternoon. See you soon."

"Bye," Tabitha said.

As Jaclyn walked away, she immediately felt vulnerable, and while she resisted looking in their direction, she knew Amelia and friends were still there.

To fill in time, she opened her textbook and began making notes for the first assignment, but found herself distracted by Alex's absence. Tabitha didn't hear them approach, but when the chair opposite her slid out from under the table, she knew who it was before she even looked up.

"Studying hard, I see," Amelia remarked in a condescending tone.

Tabitha looked up at her tormentor. "There's nothing wrong with wanting to do well, Amelia," she said.

Amelia grinned. "Of course, and it's so much harder for someone dumb like you, Tubby."

Tabitha shrugged. "Just go away, Amelia."

"So antisocial," Amelia accused. "Oh well, come on, girls, we have better things to do."

Tabitha watched the three girls sashay across the café and out of the door. She heaved a sigh of relief and continued her study.

* * * *

Amelia and her two friends would always follow Tabitha to the bus, whispering and snickering among themselves. Alex nearly always walked with her, but it didn't stop Amelia's bullying, only made Tabitha feel more secure. Today she didn't linger when the lecture had finished, but walked briskly down the nearly deserted corridor to the stairs. There she found Amelia lounging on the balcony railing, flanked by her two partners in crime, Petra and Dawn.

"Where's lover boy, Tubby? Left you all alone to fend for yourself? Did the fish bait smell get too much for him then?"

Tabitha mentally curled in on herself, and after a quick glance at her tormentor, ducked her head down and walked faster.

At the top of the stairs, Amelia blocked her path. "I asked you a question, Tubby. You don't pass until you answer it to my satisfaction."

Tabitha glanced around, but there was no one to help. She looked up at her tormentor. "I have no idea where he is, and why should I?" she muttered.

"Oh dear, then you don't know. I saw him on the weekend with a gorgeous, slim blonde. They were holding hands, all smoochy smoochy."

Tabitha tried hard to absorb the shock of Amelia's words. She kept her face as blank as she could manage because Tabitha didn't want Amelia to know her information had upset her. "Well, Alex is allowed to be smoochy with whoever he likes. We're only friends," Tabitha stated, trying hard to keep the tremor out of her voice. They were only friends, but she liked Alex, a lot.

Amelia began to laugh. "Only friends, I'll bet, but maybe you wanted more, Tubby."

"Shut up, Amelia, just shut up," Tabitha shouted as she pushed past her tormentor and hurried down the stairs.

"Awww, poor Tubby." Amelia chortled, leaning back on the rails to balance herself.

Terrified Amelia was right behind her, Tabitha ran all the way to the bus stop. When the bus pulled up Tabitha threw herself up the steps, staggered down the corridor and fell into one of the back seats. With shaking hands, she covered her burning face. Why did she let that bitch get to her so? She wasn't dating Alex, so it shouldn't matter if he dated someone else. Besides he had probably had lots of girlfriends, he was, after all, twenty-two years old. But of course Amelia's taunts had stabbed her right in her heart as they always had. It was probably all a lie anyway, but Tabitha wondered what Alex actually thought about her. She couldn't ask, but she could inquire where he was, as a friend. She immediately typed a message and sent it.

Missed you in class today, hope u r ok.

There was no reply by the time she got off at her stop and she had begun to feel embarrassed for having sent the text. Her phone beeped as she unlocked the front door. She grabbed it out of her pocket and checked the screen. Despite the fact that she didn't recognize the number, she did recognize the message.

Did he reply, Tubby? LOL.

She felt sick. How had Amelia gotten her number? She had changed it at the end of the school year. And how did Amelia know she'd messaged Alex? Tabitha was suddenly stricken by a wave of humiliation, even though she expected that Amelia was only guessing about the text. She dumped her bag in the corner, picked up her cat and lay curled up on the bed, trying not to think of Alex with another girl. They had known each other through the car club for about four years and he'd never shown any interest in her, and Tabitha didn't think he would because he was almost four years older than her—he probably thought of her as a kid.

* * * *

Alex was absent from class again on Thursday, and he still hadn't replied to her message. She'd begun to worry about him now, especially as Leo shook his head at her questioning look when she entered the room. She turned to her desk. There was a big note lying folded in the middle. High-pitched sniggers came from behind her. Tentatively she picked the note up and opened it. The words almost jumped off the paper, big, bold and uppercase.

YOU'RE GOING TO FAIL, FISHBAIT. GIVE UP NOW.

The words stabbed at her as if they were physical weapons and her hands trembled as she scrunched the note up into a tiny ball and stuffed it into her bag. Her stomach burned with the acid of anxiety as she slumped into her seat. Smothered giggles from the back of the room taunted her, but she refused to turn around and confront them. Her greatest fear was to fail.

She could barely concentrate on the lecture, unsettled by the presence of the venomous note in the bottom of her bag, and on top of that, she felt guilty leaving early just in case she missed something important. She was determined not to fail, and there was no reason to think she should, but now that Amelia had put the thought into her head, she struggled to get rid of it. Mrs. Waldrop got quite short with her when she had to repeat herself about the new stock three times. Tabitha sagged with relief when she finally arrived home, but she had barely changed and settled on her bed to flick through her playlist when her father bellowed from down the hall.

"Phone for you."

She sighed and rolled off the bed. *Who's calling me at this time of night, damn it?*

"Tabitha, phone," her father called again. "It's Alex."

An unexpected bubble of warmth exploded inside and she skipped down the hall and grabbed the handset.

"Hello," she said.

"Have you missed me?" Alex asked.

"Yes, I did. What've you been up to?"

"I got chucked off my horse in track work. Busted my head, and my phone. I've just got out of hospital."

"Oh, Alex, that's terrible. Are you okay now?" she asked.

"Yeah, I'm all good, just concussion. Are you still on for study Saturday?" Alex asked. "I'll need to catch up."

A wave of relief washed over her. Alex had been hurt, not out dating someone else, and he still wanted to come over. "Yeah, sure. I've got lots of notes."

"Okay, great. Can I come earlier than two? I'm not allowed

24

to ride for another week."

"No problems, Alex, come any time after ten. We can get some takeaway, or make a sandwich or something here."

"Great, whatever is easiest. Do you have any ideas for assignment one?"

"I do. What about you?"

"Been too crook to think about it," Alex muttered.

"What about the stables, you know, training racehorses or something."

"I know, we have a big gelding, Firefly Dusk, he's recovering from injury. It's pretty involved. That might work."

"Sounds good, Alex. I am sure we can get it sorted together. So see you Saturday before lunch."

"Yep. Looking forward to it."

"Bye," she said as the connection was broken.

A warm sensation of satisfaction bubbled up inside. She hugged herself. Alex was still going to be her study mate.

* * * *

It was almost eleven when Tabitha heard Alex's car pull into the drive. She bounced down the passage and opened the door.

"Hiya. All ready to work?" Alex asked as he climbed slowly up onto the veranda.

Tabitha smiled. "Yes, if you are. How's the head?"

Alex tipped his head to the side and parted his hair above his ear. "Six stitches and a big egg," he said.

She leaned in to inspect his injury. It looked painful and she shuddered, but at the same time, she was aware of his smell. It was nice, spicy almost. She took a deep breath and felt her skin tingle all over with awareness. "You're so lucky, Alex, you didn't get really hurt," she said, stepping back hastily.

He smiled. "Yeah. Dad says I'm too hardheaded to come to any real harm."

Tabitha loved his smile, slightly crooked and cheeky. It sent shivers down her spine. "Is it dangerous, riding racehorses?" she asked, leading the way into the family room.

Alex followed her. "Nah. Well, mostly not, but jockeys get hurt sometimes. They say there's more chance of getting hurt in the car, though."

"Be careful, won't you, Alex?" she said.

He grinned. "I didn't know you cared." He gave a mock bow in her direction.

"Of course I care, Alex...I..." Her face felt hot, all of a sudden. "I mean that...Well, friends are supposed to care, aren't they?" she stuttered, and moved toward the kitchen in an effort to hide her embarrassment. "Do you want a coffee?" she asked.

"Yeah," Alex replied as he spread his books out beside hers.

They worked through the notes from the classes Alex had missed. Tabitha found she understood them better after she'd explained it all to Alex.

"That's better, it makes sense now," she said and closed her notebook. "Do you want some lunch? I can make sandwiches and we can eat outside on the deck if you like?"

Alex hovered in the kitchen, making Tabitha nervous. She really liked him, but she had no idea how he felt, and as they were good friends already, she didn't want to do anything to spoil that.

Alex perched on the end of the bench, swinging his legs back and forth. "So, Tabitha, is Amelia still bugging you?"

She shrugged. "Yes, but she's been doing it since preschool. I don't expect her to stop any time soon."

"She never lets up, does she? You sure you don't want me and Leo to shut her up?" he asked, making a mock savage face.

Tabitha shook her head, not sure what to say, as she struggled with her surprise at Alex's offer. "It's probably best if I just ignore it. That's what everyone says."

Alex followed her outside, bringing a bottle of soft drink and glasses with him.

Alex munched on his sandwich for a while, then he said, "We should go riding sometime."

Tabitha gulped, chewed her sandwich and swallowed hastily before she choked on her mouthful. "On the racehorses?" she blurted.

Alex laughed out loud, his brown eyes sparkling and slightly crooked front teeth showing. "Hell, no. I know where you can hire some tame nags. Have you ridden before?"

Tabitha shook her head. "What if I fall off?" she asked.

Alex reached out and patted her hand. "Then you get straight back on."

Sparks flew between his skin and hers. But before she could react, his touch was gone. She took a deep, shuddering breath.

Alex looked concerned. "You don't have to, you know, Tabitha, it was just a thought."

She smiled. "I'd like to give it a try, Alex, really. I think horses are so beautiful."

"Good, wait till the holidays, then we'll go. Now, assignment one, I think."

By the time Alex left, they both had rough outlines of assignment one, his on the stables, hers on the vet clinic. Tabitha waved Alex off, feeling happy inside for the first time in a long while. She was even looking forward to college on Tuesday.

* * * *

Monday morning her phone beeped. She grabbed it, hoping it might be Alex suggesting they get together. It wasn't. The message was blunt.

U gonna fail, bitch.

Tabitha shivered. *Damn Amelia.* The phone beeped three

27

more times. All with the same message. Tabitha switched her phone off and concentrated on her assignment. She had no intention of failing, regardless of what Amelia said.

* * * *

Tabitha felt happy with her completed assignment when she submitted it. Amelia, sitting at the back of the room, just shook her head in Tabitha's direction as she resumed her seat. Alex slipped into the seat beside her and Tabitha heard Amelia snicker.

Tabitha leaned over to Alex. "Amelia's laughing at me because she thinks I'm going to fail," she whispered.

Alex glared over his shoulder before he brought his mouth close to Tabitha's ear. "Ignore it. I saw the draft of your assignment, it was good."

"I can't help but feel worried, Alex," she moaned.

"Don't stress. She's just a stupid cow and you need to have faith in yourself," Alex replied.

Slightly mollified by Alex's reaction, Tabitha settled down to concentrate on the tutorial about canine body language.

After an enjoyable lunch with Alex and Jaclyn, she quickly ducked into the toilet on the way back to class.

As she shut the door, she heard someone enter the bathroom and voices whispering. She cringed back in the stall as she heard Amelia's voice.

"I heard she got Alex to help her. She was really floundering. Wonder how she rewarded him…" Female laughter rattled around the tiled bathroom.

"Well, we'd better leave her one of these, just in case," Amelia said loudly, then the door squeaked and silence enveloped the room.

Tabitha opened the door just a crack. The outer space was empty. Hurriedly she slipped out of the cubicle and went to wash her hands. She stood stunned. By each of the basins lay a pregnancy test box. Nausea washed over her. She didn't know whether to snatch them up, hide them, bin them or walk away and pretend she hadn't seen them. Whichever choice she made it would be wrong. As she stared at the offending items, wishing they would vanish, the door squeaked and two girls she didn't know pushed in. They immediately saw what Tabitha was looking at. They snickered.

"They yours?" the blonde one asked.

Tabitha shook her head. "No, they were just here when I came out of the loo."

"You're sure there're not yours? You probably only need one anyway." The redhead with the razor cut giggled as she headed for the cubicle.

"I don't need any," Tabitha protested.

The girls just tittered and disappeared.

Tabitha's face was searing. She looked at her reflection, her blush turning a deeper red as humiliation raged through her. In the end she heaved a deep sigh, snatched the boxes from the basins and shoved them in her bag. She snuck into class late, again, and Kayne gave her a stern look of disapproval as she tiptoed quietly to her desk. Alex frowned a query at her as Kayne resumed the lecture. Smothered sniggering that could just be heard by everyone came from the back of the room. Tabitha shook her head in response to Alex, twisted her mouth into a look of distaste and indicated Amelia with a slight tilt of her head. Alex's frown deepened but he didn't comment until the end of class.

As Tabitha stood to leave, he took hold of her arm and pulled her back down in her seat.

"Wait, Tabitha."

Amelia lurked by the door for a long moment, but finally left when she realized they weren't moving.

"What did she do this time?" Alex asked.

Tabitha shook her head. "It doesn't matter, Alex, now let's go home."

Alex touched her arm. "It does matter, Tabitha. Obviously it's upset you."

She shrugged. "I can't talk about it."

"Come on, Tabitha, spit it out."

Tabitha pulled away from him and jumped to her feet. "No, Alex, I can't—it's too personal."

Alex stared up at her, his expression clearly showing his frustration with her answer.

"Fine then, don't tell me," he replied, picking up his bag as he stood. "Let's go."

Tabitha trailed after him, awash with a mixture of embarrassment and regret. She felt like she'd let her friend down by refusing to reveal Amelia's latest assault, but how could she wave a pregnancy test under Alex's nose? He could read so much into the item, and it could destroy the comfortable companionship between them. Sex could be such a touchy issue, and not one Tabitha felt comfortable talking to Alex about.

They walked side by side to the bus in uneasy silence.

As they reached the bus shelter, Alex turned to her. "You sure you don't want to tell me, Tabitha?"

She shook her head, cringing inside. "It's too embarrassing, Alex, really…"

"We're friends, Tabitha." He sounded hurt by her refusal to fess up.

"I know, Alex, but you're a boy."

He stared at her for a moment then burst into raucous laughter. "A boy, is it? Well, then, that's put me in my place."

Tabitha felt the heat rushing up her face. "Well, a man then…" She stopped speaking and looked down at her feet, all too aware of the four years between them and wondering if at twenty-two he found her immature. Especially when she didn't stand up to Amelia.

Alex put a finger under her chin and lifted her face so she had to look directly into his eyes. "You tie yourself up in such knots, my dear little Kitty Kat, but never mind, I gather it is a 'girl' thing so I'll let you off this time, but you need to learn to trust me, Tabitha, because we're mates."

She nodded. "I'm glad we're mates, Alex."

* * * *

Tabitha fretted overnight about her parting from Alex. He had seemed okay in the end that she refused to tell, but she worried it had damaged his opinion of her. She really liked him, and wanted more than friendship, but she didn't want to lose that either, and with him being so much older, she doubted he was interested in a kid like her.

Fortunately she was kept fairly busy all day Wednesday at the vet clinic, helping the head vet, Harriet, birth five kittens to a battered, half-starved, half-grown cat they'd found on the doorstep in the morning. The mother was in such poor condition they immediately started hand feeding the kittens to supplement what little milk the mother could supply. It was Tabitha's job to do the feeding, toileting and general care of the kittens. She didn't mind at all and was just grateful Harriet hadn't been able to bring herself to euthanize the cat and her kittens, even though their presence at the clinic added to the workload. Tabitha offered to come in every spare day she had, unpaid, to care for them. Harriet agreed to Tabitha doing the daytime feeds and the staff would manage the nighttime and early-morning ones. Tabitha knew the kitten situation would be an ideal subject for her second assignment.

* * * *

Alex was back to his old self on Thursday and made no mention of Tuesday's incident. Kayne walked slowly around the classroom and gave out the marked assignments.

"Some have done better than others, but I think in this case, it's just laziness. You do need to apply yourselves to pass this course, folks," Kayne stated.

Tabitha put her hands on top of the downturned paperwork. They trembled. She hesitated, afraid to turn it over. Alex turned his over.

31

"Hah, got a distinction," he announced. "Go on, Tabitha, you'll have passed," he muttered in her ear.

She looked at him. She could hardly breathe.

"Do it, Tabitha," Alex urged.

She picked the assignment up by the corner and flipped it over. For a brief second, she shut her eyes then opened them and looked down.

"Oh my God, I got a credit plus," she squeaked.

Alex slapped his hand down on her work. "See? I told you so. Tell you what, I'll take you riding on the weekend to celebrate our success."

"I'd like that, Alex. I'm not working this weekend, so either Saturday or Sunday."

"Make it Sunday. Aren't we studying on Saturday? I'll text you the details."

"Are we ready, people?" Kayne asked impatiently from the front of the room.

Fifteen minutes before the end of the class, Amelia left the room with a mumbled, "Need the bathroom."

She hadn't returned by the time Tabitha packed up and slipped out of the door. Her absence made Tabitha nervous as she ran lightly down the stairs and through reception, but there was no sign of her tormentor as she left the college. As she hurried down the street toward the bus, she sensed she was being followed. She turned and found Amelia walking right behind her. Even though Amelia ignored her, the familiar twisting burn of anxiety knotted Tabitha's stomach as she walked. At the bus stop, Amelia stood behind the shelter, seemingly completely oblivious of Tabitha, who perched on the very edge of the seat to wait for the bus.

Tabitha agonized over Amelia's presence. What the hell was her persecutor up to now? This was no time for a confrontation, she needed to get to work. Finally, too nervous to sit still while she waited, Tabitha paced up and down in front of the shelter and cursed the lateness of the bus. If it didn't arrive soon, she would be late, regardless of what Amelia planned. Still Amelia ignored her.

At last the bus pulled up, but as Tabitha went to board, Amelia jumped in front of her and waltzed down the aisle to the back seat. Tabitha validated her ticket and took a seat near the front. She wished she could keep an eye on Amelia, but she refused to humiliate herself by turning around to look. Petrified of what Amelia planned to do, Tabitha counted every minute of the bus journey, expecting at any moment to be attacked. Today was somehow different, because despite everything, Amelia had never followed her away from school or college before. Tabitha was convinced her nemesis had something diabolical planned. As she changed buses, Amelia switched, too, following right behind her. Still her bully said nothing. Her silent hovering seemed almost worse than the taunts.

Halfway through the journey, Tabitha couldn't stand the impasse any longer, so she turned to face her harasser. "What're you up to, Amelia? Just leave me alone."

The other girl just smiled and said quietly, "Anyone's allowed on this bus, Tubby, even someone like you."

Tabitha felt stupid. Was she paranoid now, that she thought Amelia was always after her? She hunched down in her seat, but no matter how she tried to ignore her, Amelia's presence burned a hole in her back.

Tabitha bolted off the bus without a backward glance and hurried across the car park, but as Tabitha entered the shopping center, she was acutely aware of Amelia strolling casually a few feet behind her. She hurried down the central mall expecting to be pounced on, but by the time Tabitha had reached Mrs. Waldrop's shop, Amelia had disappeared.

Once she was in the shop, she began to relax and took her place behind the counter. She must really get a hold of herself and not assume Amelia was always out to get her. As soon as she was settled, Mrs. Waldrop went out to get her afternoon coffee before she retreated, as usual, to her little alcove to do the paperwork.

Tabitha dusted shelves, unpacked some boxes of delicate

pepper and salt shakers and arranged them on a glass shelf, as per her employer's instructions. There were several customers, with one lady buying up big on bone china figurines. Mrs. Waldrop came out to help Tabitha pack them. By eight, even the mall outside the shop had emptied of most of the shoppers, and Tabitha went back to cleaning. She didn't hear her next customer come in, but at the clatter of china on the glass counter she jumped up from behind the shelves and came face to face with Amelia, along with Petra and Dawn in guard formation behind her.

Oh my God, how had Amelia found me. I haven't told anyone I'm working here.

"Ah, I wondered when I would get some service," Amelia drawled.

"What can I help you with?" Tabitha asked, struggling to keep the tremor out of her voice. Her skin tingled with apprehension. Amelia's presence in the shop could only mean trouble. *Oh, for goodness' sake stop it, she probably only wants to buy something.*

Amelia ran her hand over the four ornaments she had placed on the counter and tipped her head to one side. "I'm so undecided, you see. I need a gift for a special friend, and all four of these are so lovely. One of the bunnies, the butterfly or the girl. I just can't choose."

"Well, they're all good bone china, and you can get sets if you buy this one," Tabitha said as she touched the little apricot-colored rabbit holding the flowers. "The rabbits and the butterfly are only thirty-nine dollars each, but the little girl on the swing is seventy-nine ninety-five."

"Well, money's not a problem as it is with people like you, Tubby," Amelia said scornfully.

Tabitha cringed at Amelia's reference to her working-class background. Of course she hadn't expected pleasantries from this person, but her continuous references to lack of income was humiliating.

Idly Amelia moved each of the items around the surface of the counter. The china made soft screeching noises as it slid on the glass. Totally rattled by the unspoken threat in Amelia's actions, Tabitha pressed the little red button to summon her employer.

"Please be careful with the items, Amelia. If you break one, you will still have to pay for it," she warned.

"Really?" Amelia taunted, her eyebrows lifted into elegant arches. "And are you going to make me?"

"Just be careful?" Tabitha pleaded.

Amelia laughed an icy cackle. "No, I thought not. And what happens if the customer doesn't pay?"

"Then Mrs. Waldrop will have to claim on insurance or she might take it out of my wages," Tabitha snapped back, wishing fervently Mrs. Waldrop would come before Amelia did her worst. She pressed the button again, harder this time.

"Oh dear, that is such a shame." Amelia snickered as she slid the little girl ornament toward the edge of the counter.

"Amelia, please don't do this. It's wrong. You shouldn't hurt others just because you hate me."

Where the heck was her boss? She hardly ever left the alcove. Maybe she'd nipped out to the ladies' without telling Tabitha.

"Don't, Amelia." The three girls in front of the counter all echoed Tabitha's plea in high-pitched, childlike voices.

Amelia promptly slid the ornament farther. "Oops." She chortled as it tipped off the edge and fell to the floor. The crash of shattering bone china echoed, sharp and loud, through the shop. Pieces scuttled everywhere across the tiled floor. "Oh dear, looks like you've had an accident," Amelia said loudly.

"Amelia, you did it and you'll have to pay for it," Tabitha said as forcefully as she could manage. A wave of nausea washed over her.

Amelia scooped up her bag, swung it over her shoulder and began to march out of the shop. "You and what army, Tubby Tabby? You're so gutless you couldn't even kill a fly. Such a pathetic wuss. You can't make me do anything."

35

"Maybe she can't, but I can, young lady." Mrs. Waldrop's hand latched onto Amelia's shoulder. "That will be seventy-nine dollars and ninety-five cents."

"Like hell, old lady — she did it. Tubby's always clumsy," Amelia accused, pointing in Tabitha's direction.

"You're responsible, young lady — if one can call you such. You will pay. Now give your card to Tabitha. She will process the payment," Mrs. Waldrop replied.

"Get your hands off me, you old bag," Amelia yelled, pulling away.

But Mrs. Waldrop held her shoulder in a viselike grip. "Tabitha, call the police, please, and shopping center security."

Now Amelia really squirmed against her imprisonment. "I haven't done anything wrong. I didn't steal anything," she protested.

"You will pay for the item you willfully broke, or I will have you charged with destroying property — or some such misdemeanor. You will then have a record, young lady, and I'm sure your parents will not be pleased."

For the first time ever, Tabitha saw fear in Amelia's face.

She struggled again against the older woman's restraint. "All right, I'll pay. There's no need to call my parents or the police. I'll pay. Here." She threw her card on the counter.

Mrs. Waldrop still held her shoulder.

Dawn and Petra fled the scene, leaving their fearless leader to her fate. As Tabitha held out the EFTPOS machine to Amelia so she could enter her PIN, she glimpsed the glisten of tears in her bully's eyes. She felt a fiery sense of satisfaction to see Amelia caught out in her nastiness, but she suspected from Amelia's reaction her parents scared her more than the cops.

With the money paid, Mrs. Waldrop escorted Amelia to the door. "Now, young lady, I never want to see you in my shop again. You take your friends and conduct your shenanigans elsewhere. I do not tolerate it."

"You old bat. We wouldn't want to come back here

anyway," Amelia snarled as she shook Mrs. Waldrop's hand from her shoulder and stomped out across the mall.

"Now, Tabitha, can you clean up the mess? Then we will close early, I think we've both had enough for one night."

With the shop back in order and the surviving ornaments safely returned to their rightful shelves, Tabitha collected her bag before she helped her boss lock the doors.

"Come on, young lady. I'll give you a lift home tonight. You look a little shaken."

* * * *

Of course, Tabitha had to explain to her startled parents why she'd been given a lift home.

Her father was livid. "How dare she go to your place of employment? I've a good mind to speak to her parents. This persecution has to stop."

"Dad, just leave it, okay? You can't do anything. Nobody can," Tabitha wailed.

He must have sensed her desperation, how close she was to cracking, for he turned to Mrs. Waldrop and thanked her for her kindness.

Tabitha retreated to her bed—the one place she felt safe. She lay for a long time in the dark, reliving the humiliating scene at the shop. Her work had always been a safe place, but now her space had been violated. Mrs. Waldrop wouldn't tolerate any more episodes like tonight and Tabitha felt so responsible for the unpleasant incident and deeply resentful of the invasion of her personal space. And there was nothing to stop her turning up at the vet clinic and causing some sort of debacle there. The ache in Tabitha's heart was almost physical, it hurt so much. She wanted to howl, scream or smash something—anything to protest this torture, to protest her own inability to protect herself, to fight back, to get Amelia off her case. An undercurrent of anger also simmered inside at the failure of the adults to protect her, or to give her strategies that worked—really

37

worked. She'd tried all the tactics purported to be the way to handle a bully and the reality was none of them had much effect, especially with a persistent bully like Amelia.

She thought then of the tears she had seen hiding in her nemesis's eyes. It had not occurred to her that Amelia was afraid of something—so afraid she could be brought to tears by its mention. She'd never had anything to do with Amelia's family and couldn't remember having seen her parents at school functions, helping out with excursions or reading in class. For that matter, she wondered now if they had even been at the fateful ballet concert that had started Amelia's vendetta against her. Amelia's parents had definitely not fought for her right to be a fairy like her own mother had. All Tabitha knew about Amelia's family was she had three older brothers and her father was chief executive officer of some big company. They had plenty of money, apparently.

The thoughts slipped away—she didn't have head space for Amelia's issues right now. Somehow she had to get her head around Amelia's ability to destroy her equilibrium. Tabitha was weary—in fact exhausted—of always being on the lookout, constantly on the defensive. Of wilting under the unrelenting burden of humiliation she carried around day and night. Most mornings she struggled with the prospect of facing another battle. Even when Amelia was not right there in her face, Tabitha wrestled with self-preservation. She kept her guard up all the time, distancing herself from people just in case they decided to insult her. Most often those insults didn't come, but Tabitha remained wary.

She jumped when her phone beeped on the bedside table. Instead of being an enjoyable communication device, the phone had become a source of torment all its own. She couldn't bring herself to turn it off and lose contact with her social network, but its presence brought Amelia right in her pocket every time it beeped, even if it wasn't one of her demeaning texts. As she read the message, the tension flowed out of her—it was Jaclyn inviting her to catch up at the Plaza Friday afternoon.

She messaged back, making the catch-up for lunch as she had to come back and feed the kittens in the afternoon. Another small life raft to cling to—to get her through another day. But despite these highlights, Tabitha was sinking. Like the *Titanic*, holed by bullying and filling fast with misery, self-loathing and inadequacy. She was acutely aware that out of that hole also poured all that made her Tabitha—her compassion, her sense of humor, her love of life and her rapport with animals. Soon there would be nothing left but an empty shell. Tabitha didn't want to be dead inside. Alex wouldn't be interested in her if she was dead inside. In the quiet darkness of her room, she decided she could not live as a victim, always on the defensive, but she couldn't come up with any workable solution to her problem.

* * * *

She liked Jaclyn and tried to put a positive front on as she met her by the bus interchange. They walked to the Plaza and found a quiet corner in the food court. It was pretty busy so it took a while to get served, but finally each with their favorite food, they settled down to catch up. For a while they talked about their study and their respective successes with their first assignments.

Jaclyn suddenly leaned closer to Tabitha. "Tabitha, I'm your friend, right?"

Tabitha smiled in agreement.

"I've heard whispers at college, about you and Alex. That Petra girl is friends with Melody, in my class. She's been saying you're…" Jaclyn looked down and fiddled with the wrappers from her food. Her face flushed pink when she looked back up at Tabitha. "They're saying you're a slut, and you're pregnant to Alex."

Tabitha stared at Jaclyn. Speech refused to form as a terrible numbness took hold of her mind. Jaclyn reached

39

out and touched her hand, but Tabitha snatched it away from her friend's consoling touch. She clenched her two hands together to hide the trembling.

"I am not... I have not...Alex is only a friend," she stuttered.

"I knew it was a lie, but I thought you should know what they're saying," Jaclyn replied.

Now Tabitha reached out to Jaclyn. "It's all right, Jaclyn, it's not your fault."

"That Amelia girl is such a bitch. She really has it in for you," Jaclyn announced.

Tabitha shrugged. "Since I was five..." Tabitha's words faded as tears threatened to overwhelm her. How could she live with this new embarrassment and his? Poor Alex. She didn't care so much for herself, she was used to being insulted, but Alex was a different matter. Surely he was going to run a mile now—even from being friends. *And I don't blame him one bit.*

"Come on, let's go round to that shop with the costume jewelry. I heard they're having a sale and they've got some great stuff."

Tabitha dredged up a smile. "Sure, why not. I might even buy myself something."

"A bit of bling to cheer you up," Jaclyn said.

Together they browsed the racks.

"Here, look at this. It would suit that blue jumper you wore last week."

Tabitha smiled and took the necklace Jaclyn proffered. "It will. Does it have earrings to match?"

Two racks down they found a pair of blue earrings. Tabitha took them while Jaclyn took a green pair with gold trimmings. After they'd paid for their purchases, they went for a milkshake.

"You're not mad at me, about the gossip?"

Tabitha shook her head. "No, of course not. I'm just worried what Alex will think. It's embarrassing."

Jaclyn nodded. "It is, but he's not some kid—isn't he a bit

older than us?"

"Quite a bit and that makes it worse—he's just going to think we're all immature."

Jaclyn smiled. "You like him, don't you?"

Heat rushed into Tabitha's face. She peered deeply into her milkshake.

"Hey, there's nothing wrong with that. I think he's a lovely guy and good looking."

Tabitha looked at her new friend. "He is, but he's never going to see me as an equal—not now, with that ghastly rumor going around."

Jaclyn reached out and touched her hand. "Try not to get too stressed, see what happens."

"It's so unfair. Anyway, Jac, I'd better go and feed these kittens. You don't want one, do you?"

Jaclyn shook her head as she stood to go. "No, Mum thinks the dog is more than enough."

* * * *

Tabitha stewed about the ugly rumor and her study session with Alex, right up until he walked in the door and chucked his books on the table. They went together and fed the kittens. Tabitha could hardly keep her eyes off Alex as he nursed the tiny little furballs, making sure they sucked their milk and wiping their bottoms after. He was so spunky, all six foot two of his lean frame. His red tee clung to his muscular chest and his tanned arms were exposed by the short sleeves. His dark hair hung down over his forehead as he watched a kitten feed, his long legs stretched out, his sneakered feet resting on a box.

He looked across at her and smiled. "They're so tiny, cute. Their eyes aren't even open yet," he said, holding his up to inspect it.

"Yeah they're cute, but they can really make a racket when they're hungry. I hope Harriett can find homes for them. She said she would desex and vaccinate them before they were adopted."

"Maybe I could take one to the stables. Fred's always complaining of mice in the hay shed," Alex suggested.

"What about the horses? Wouldn't they tread on it?" Tabitha asked.

Alex looked across at her. "Nah. We had a cat before, it died of old age. Some of the horses really liked that old cat, and I would be there every day to look after it."

"Okay. I'd like to take one home too, but we already have a cat and I don't think Dad would approve. Anyway, we've finished here, best get back home to the study."

"Definitely, you've got to top that credit plus with your second assignment."

She shrugged. "Maybe."

Alex grinned down at her as he held the car door open. "No maybe about it. You're going to make a great vet nurse."

Warm sensation washed over her. It was nice that Alex believed in her and she didn't want to let him down. *I will pass this course – not just for him but for me.*

* * * *

As they settled at the table, Alex fiddled with his books before he looked up. "Tabitha, there's been rumors about you, well, about us, actually, going around the college."

Tabitha's face began to burn. "I know, Jaclyn told me yesterday. I'm sorry, Alex, that you've been targeted. It's so embarrassing, I'll understand if you don't want to be my friend anymore." Her throat tightened as she strangled her tears down. She didn't want to lose Alex as her friend, but she needed to give him an out. It was only fair, for Amelia's spite toward Tabitha was not his problem.

He laughed then. "Come on, we both know it's not true. So I get a bit of stick from a couple of my less mature mates, so what? We're friends, and friends don't pike over a bit of nasty gossip. I just brought it up to make sure we're good."

Tabitha silently stared at Alex. She could hardly

42

comprehend his attitude. Her heart fluffed up and thumped with an irregular beat of joy.

"Smile, Tabitha. We're good, yes?"

She nodded and smiled. "Yes, Alex, we're good."

Tabitha squashed down her own discomfort when Alex didn't show any and they worked through the assignment, bouncing ideas back and forth until they both had good drafts finished.

It wasn't until after Alex left that doubts began to creep in. Of course he wasn't upset about the rumor. None of his mates would believe it anyway—him dating a kid like her. They would all probably just find it amusing. It was best they remained just friends, and anyway the gossip would blow over eventually. She would hug her fledgling feelings for Alex to herself and enjoy his friendship. She desperately hoped she wouldn't make a fool of herself when they went riding. Excitement and nervousness harried her until she fell asleep, exhausted.

* * * *

With her second assignment finished, Tabitha didn't have a guilty conscience as they saddled the horses.

Alex came around and stood by her horse. "Up you go, Tabitha."

She looked at the stirrup then back at Alex. She wasn't sure how to manage the mount with any dignity.

Alex grinned. "It's a long way up, here. I'll give you a leg up."

Tabitha looked at his cupped hands in horror. He expected her to step into his hands and climb up into the saddle. She was no lightweight and was immediately self-conscious, but without making a fuss, there was no way out.

She lifted her foot and placed it in his hands then, gripping the saddle, she hopped and tried to get high enough to swing her leg over.

Then she was tumbling. Alex's hands were gone and she

thumped hard with both feet onto the ground, stumbling and losing her balance. Alex grabbed her shoulders and steadied her as she fell against his chest. Her breasts were squashed against his hard muscles and his scent wafted over her.

"Oops," he muttered in her ear, making no attempt to push her away.

"Sorry, Alex," she murmured into his shoulder, trying to hide the flaming humiliation that heated her face.

"Ah, my fault, didn't give you enough of a boost," he said.

She looked up into his smiling eyes and found herself drowning in the dark depths. Awareness of their closeness washed over her. For a split second, they stood unmoving, him stared down into her eyes and Tabitha, transfixed, stared up into his.

With a sudden rush of nerves, Tabitha pushed away from him, breaking the spell. She struggled to breathe evenly as she turned back to the horse. Alex didn't say anything, just held out his cupped hands again. This time, with a good boost from Alex, Tabitha landed with the slightest of bumps in the saddle. Alex immediately took her hands and placed them correctly on the reins.

"How's that, Tabitha?" he asked as he smiled up at her, his hand moving from hers down to rest on her thigh.

Tabitha settled in the saddle, trying to ignore the sizzling warmth from his palm through her leggings. She felt all warm and fuzzy inside. "All good, Alex."

His hand slipped away and a moment later he popped up into the saddle of the second horse. They rode at a walk down the driveway and through the gate into a large, flat paddock.

"How do you feel, Tabitha? Secure?" Alex asked.

"This is great," she said, smiling across at him.

Her body was still tingling with awareness from his closeness, and as she rode she admired him, how easy and relaxed he was in the saddle, almost moving as one with the horse. Tabitha thought he should have had a stockman's whip on the saddle and an Akubra hat instead of the helmet on his head. She wondered if he had been affected like she had when she fell against him. He hadn't pushed her away, and she had thought for a moment he might kiss her. Part of her had wanted him to kiss her, the other part had been terrified it might actually happen. Then again, maybe he wasn't interested in kissing her at all. Maybe she'd imagined it because she wanted him to.

Under Alex's guidance she learned how to trot, and as they moved up a steady slope, he encouraged her to canter. It was exhilarating, with the horse moving under her, the thud of the hooves and the wind in her face. Alex pulled up on the crest.

He grinned. "It's good, isn't it?" he asked.

"I'm really enjoying myself," she replied.

Alex turned his horse and headed over the crest and Tabitha followed him as he rode down the other side of the hill and into a small gully overhung with huge white gum trees. He dismounted and tied up his horse. Tabitha followed suit. Her legs felt funny, almost numb as she went to step forward and nearly lost her balance.

Alex chuckled as he grabbed her arm. "Got a sore bum, have we?"

"It's not funny, Alex," Tabitha grumbled, giving his arm a slap.

He laughed out loud now. "Oh, come on, I'll help you," he said, immediately wrapping his arm around her waist and pulling her close to him.

Overcome with a rush of shyness, Tabitha fought the urge to protest his assistance and allowed him to embrace her waist as they walked slowly down the slope. It was shady and cool under the trees by the stream that gurgled cheerfully over the narrow, rocky bed.

Alex turned to face her. "What do you think, Tabitha? This is one of my favorite places."

She looked up at him, acutely aware that his hand still rested on her waist. "It's beautiful, and peaceful."

He looked down at her, his gaze focused first on her eyes, then her mouth. He moved closer. His scent wafted and intermingled with her flowery perfume. An intoxicating mix. His eyes were dark and soft, his mouth curved up into a smile. He slid his hands up her arms, across her shoulders, and cupped her face. His thumbs lightly caressed along her jawbone. She stood, fixated by him. Warmth radiated through her from where his hands touched her and her stomach turned dizzying somersaults. As his face filled her view, she let her eyes slide closed. She held her breath as she sensed his closeness. Then his mouth touched hers, so light it almost wasn't there. Her breath jerked and stuttered, every nerve ending dancing. Then he was moving back from her, only a small distance. Oh my God, he'd kissed her. Her first kiss. *Oh my God*. Tabitha stared up at him. She didn't know what to do, or say. She felt all warm and fuzzy.

He smiled down at her before he dove in and dropped a lightning-quick kiss on the tip of her nose. "My beautiful Tabitha," he said.

"I'm not beautiful, silly," Tabitha replied.

Alex frowned. "You are so, and I don't want to hear you say that again, okay?" he admonished as he held out his hand.

Tabitha wrinkled her nose. "I promise," she said as she clasped his hand and they walked slowly along the stream. They practiced skimming flat rocks across a still pool and Alex tried to tickle a trout they saw. All his efforts got him was wet. He took his tee off and tucked it in his belt and Tabitha couldn't keep her eyes off his buff body.

Back at the horses, after he had put his tee back on, he pulled her into his arms and kissed her again, a little more firmly and longer this time. Tabitha tingled all over. She liked the taste of him, the gentle caress of his lips against hers and the feel of his arms holding her close. Then he put her from him and looked directly into her eyes. "I think I like kissing you, Tabitha," he said softly.

She smiled. "I like it too," she said, her face warming with

46

a wave of shyness.

Alex grinned. "Good," he said. "Do you need a leg up?"

With them both mounted, Alex pointed to the tree at the top of the rise. "I'll race ya," he shouted and took off up the hill.

* * * *

She had gone in early to feed the kittens, missed the bus and was running late for class. Kayne had already started when she slipped into her seat beside Alex. Kayne waited a moment for her to get settled, but didn't say anything.

Alex frowned and mouthed, "Kittens?"

She nodded.

Amelia kept her distance during lunch, but when Jaclyn went to leave Amelia, Petra and Melody followed her. Tabitha immediately felt uneasy.

"I'm going to check on Jaclyn," Tabitha said as she jumped out of her chair. Alex was right behind her when she pushed her way through the door. The corridor was empty. Tabitha hurried up the stairs in the direction of Jaclyn's afternoon class.

She had reached the second landing before she heard their voices. The three girls surrounded Jaclyn. They were pushing her and crowding her.

"You don't need Fishbait for a mate, Jaclyn. That loser is bad for your reputation," Amelia sneered.

"Tabitha's my friend," Jaclyn cried.

They crowded close and jostled her again. "Wrong answer, Jaclyn," Amelia snarled close to Jaclyn's face.

"Leave me alone, you're all vicious bitches," Jaclyn yelled, trying to escape their enclosure.

"Awww, she has a temper," Amelia screeched.

Side by side, Alex and Tabitha raced down the passage.

"Back off, you lot," Alex shouted.

Amelia looked over her shoulder.

"Leave her alone, Amelia," Tabitha cried, grabbing at her

47

tormentor's shoulder.

"Now here's trouble--the cavalry has arrived. Let's go, girls, we'll deal with Little Miss Jaclyn later."

"Don't even think about it, you three, or else," Alex threatened.

Amelia laughed, a sharp, high bark that ended abruptly as she leaned into Tabitha's face. "You'll pay for this, Fishbait," she snarled.

Tabitha slapped out with both hands, but Amelia was already out of her reach, following her cohorts back down the stairs. Tabitha and Alex escorted Jaclyn to her class. She didn't say much, but brushed off Tabitha's apologies and hurriedly pushed through the door into her classroom.

"Poor Jaclyn. There was no reason for Amelia to pick on her," Tabitha moaned.

"No. Poor girl looked terrified," Alex said.

"She was and she wouldn't accept my apologies. Maybe she won't want to be friends anymore. And I wouldn't blame her either."

Alex hugged her. "Hey, don't go jumping to conclusions. Now come on, we have assignments to submit."

Amelia and her mates were already seated, heads bent over pages. Tabitha felt a real sense of pleasure to slip into her seat without harassment. Kayne immediately began on the new section, refusing to take any questions about the assignment, saying it was too late. She looked across at Alex and grinned. He patted his assignment and grinned back.

The subject matter was complicated and Kayne handed out a booklet with extra information. Tabitha's head was spinning and she was glad when the afternoon class finished ten minutes early because Kayne was called to the office. She went up and put her assignment with the others on the front desk as instructed. Alex put his on top, then Leo.

Amelia was still fiddling around with Dawn by the printer, trying to get their assignments finished. Leo and Alex both walked with her to the bus.

* * * *

Still riding on a high from the previous day because Harriet had offered her another day once a fortnight at the clinic, Tabitha bounced into the classroom and claimed her desk. She was barely seated when Kayne called her into his office. His handsome face was marred by a frown that drew his eyebrows down and made deep furrows above his nose. Tabitha felt that familiar acid burn of fear in her stomach. *What the hell have I done to make him mad?*

"Tabitha, I'm very disappointed with you. I want a very good reason why you failed to hand in your assignment Tuesday."

"But I did hand it in, Kayne, just before I left class," she protested. "You'd gone to the office." Every nerve ending stabbed her and her gut lurched and clenched. Where was her assignment?

"Well, it's not here, Tabitha. You know failure to hand in on time, without an official extension, is an automatic fail," Kayne said. There was a no-nonsense firmness to his tone.

"But I handed it in. I put it with all the others." She was almost wailing by this time.

"Then why don't I have it? I don't want to fail you, Tabitha, but the rules are—"

"I can't fail. I can't, and I did hand it in," she replied, wringing her hands in front of her.

"If you can prove it—"

Tabitha cut him off. "I can. Ask Alex and Leo. They put theirs on top of mine, and we left the college together. Amelia and a couple of the girls were still here, mucking around with the printer."

"Ask Alex to come in, please," Kayne instructed, but he didn't look happy.

She did, then sat at her desk with her bag still zipped. The sniggering behind her seemed loud and harsh, but she was too afraid to look around—afraid she would leap out of her chair, charge at Amelia and scratch her eyes out. She

49

huffed at herself. *Yeah, right. As if I'd have the courage.* It was obvious to her that Amelia was the only one who would have taken her assignment.

Alex returned to his seat and Leo was called into the office. He reached out and squeezed her hand. "It'll be okay, Kitty Kat," he whispered.

Half the class time was over when Kayne grudgingly gave her permission to reprint her assignment and hand it directly to him. As he took it, he warned her she would be docked forty-five percent of the overall mark. She could still pass, but that was all, no matter how good her assignment actually was. Gutted by the unfairness of it, a righteous anger seethed inside, especially when Kayne dismissed her suggestion that Amelia might know about her missing assignment. He advised her to always hand her assignments directly to him in the future, just in case they got lost. He made no attempt to take the issue further.

Tabitha couldn't hide her tears from Alex when she returned to her desk after resubmitting her assignment. He tried to comfort her and she was grateful for his efforts, but she was beyond consoling. She'd worked so hard.

"Do you want me to take you home, Tabitha?" he asked softly.

She shook her head. "No thanks, neither of us can afford to miss this stuff, it's complicated."

"You sure? I can hear her sniggering back there."

Tabitha looked up at him through tear-filled eyes. "Let her snigger, I'm not going to run away."

Alex squeezed her hand. "Good one, Kitty Kat. You know you're much stronger than you give yourself credit for."

She sniffed. "I don't feel strong."

He squeezed her hand again and turned back to the lecture.

But it wasn't until Alex had left her at the bus stop that the real coldness of reality settled in her soul. The reality that Amelia could make her fail. Locked in her own misery, she muddled through the process of feeding the kittens, not

50

lingering to cuddle them as she normally did, and she was glad to find her mother out when she finally shut the door behind her and stomped up the passage to the sanctuary of her room.

* * * *

The shrill ring of her phone tore her from sleep. With a shaky hand, she reached out to grab it, but by the time she put it to her ear, the caller had hung up. Tabitha looked at the time—three a.m. She didn't need to see the number to know who it was. With a sigh of resignation, she turned her phone off and lay back down, already sinking into a black hole of misery. Damn Amelia. Her sense of self and what little confidence she had was gradually being eroded by the constant tap, tap of Amelia's bullying. She felt isolated from her 'crowd' because she wasn't game to go on Facebook or any of the other social media sites, but her greatest fear was that Alex would get sick of the constant barrage of insults and the way she crept around. He told her often she had to stand up for herself and she tried, but the torment continued. She didn't know how long she could go on doing this.

Her sleep was light and broken as she tossed and turned, alternating between bad dreams dominated by Amelia and lying awake, fretting about her future. By dawn she'd had enough of pretending to sleep and, ignoring her burning eyes and aching muscles, climbed out of bed and went for a walk. When she returned she felt more awake, but no more prepared to face the onslaught of text messages that had flooded her phone during the night. If it weren't for Alex and Jaclyn contacting her, she would turn the damn thing off and leave it off. She braced herself to open the first one.

Don't think that was the end of it, Fishbait, you smelly slut

She cringed at the cruel words. There were fifty from the same number. She deleted the remainder without opening

51

them. Not that it helped, for she already knew what each contained, and it hurt just knowing they had once existed, and while she didn't intend for the cruelty to sap her energy, it did. She wished she had not agreed to do an extra shift at Mrs. Waldrop's. But with Alex away at a country race meeting all weekend, it was a chance to add to her car savings.

When the shop phone rang, she picked it up. "Mrs. Waldrop's Unique Gifts, Tabitha speaking."

The heavy breathing coming down the line sent shivers down her skin.

"Mrs. Waldrop's Unique Gifts, Tabitha speaking. Can I help you?"

There was a peal of raucous laughter and the click of the phone being disconnected.

"Who was that, Tabitha?"

Tabitha smiled. "Just a wrong number, Mrs. Waldrop."

Her employer nodded.

The phone rang again. Tabitha jumped in nervous anticipation. She picked up the phone. "Mrs. Waldrop's Unique Gifts, Tabitha speaking. Can I help you?"

Again the loud, almost hysterical cackling rattled in her ear Tabitha quietly put the phone down.

Mrs. Waldrop looked over at her. "Again?" she asked.

Tabitha nodded.

"Wretched people—too lazy to look up the correct number," Mrs. Waldrop snapped.

Tabitha had just finished wrapping a gift selection for a regular customer when the phone shrilled again. Tabitha jumped, almost dropping her parcel. She handed the item to the customer and smiled goodbye before she picked up the receiver.

"Mrs. Waldrop's Unique Gifts, Tabitha speaking. Can I help you?"

"She mad yet, Fishbait?" Amelia asked, then began to laugh.

Mrs. Waldrop's hand closed over the phone. "I'll take

this, Tabitha," she said.

Tabitha let go of the phone and stepped back, anxiety tearing her to shreds as she heard Amelia's laughter echo out of the hand piece.

"I think that is sufficient, you nasty little troublemaker. Another call and I'll have the police onto you and your parents. I have your details."

Tabitha heard the phone crash down on the other end of the line.

Mrs. Waldrop turned to Tabitha, her mouth pursed into a thin line. "Tabitha, I realize this is not your fault, but if there is one more incident like that, I will have to let you go. I'm sorry, but my nerves just won't stand it."

Tabitha stared at her employer, the sting of tears burning her eyeballs. "I'm so sorry, Mrs. Waldrop, I haven't encouraged her. Please don't sack me."

Mrs. Waldrop shook her head. "You haven't discouraged her either, Tabitha. You need to get this girl off your back. I'm really sorry, you're an excellent worker, and an honest young woman, but I just cannot be expected to cope with such harassment."

"I know, Mrs. Waldrop, but I just don't know what to do."

"You will need to figure it out, Tabitha. You have one more chance, only because I like you, but after that, I'm sorry. I won't say any more about it for now so I suggest you get on with dusting the back shelves while I rearrange the window display."

Tabitha nodded. "Yes, Mrs. Waldrop," she said as she picked up the dusting cloth. She fought back the tears that filled her eyes. Her heart raced at the thought of losing this job, especially as she had worked so hard to be the best employee. She took her time, being extra careful with the dainty bone china crockery, aware her trembling hands could lose their grip without warning.

She sagged with relief when she finally knocked off and caught the bus. She turned her phone on. There was a list of messages and her voicemail was full. She looked at the first message, knowing it was from Amelia.

Did you get busted, Fishbait? The old bag sounded mad.

Tears ran down her cheeks as she deleted the rest of the messages, knowing they would all be the same. She didn't even listen to her voicemail, just deleted all but the two from Alex. She opened up the first.

"Hey, Kitty Kat, guess you're working. Just letting you know all is good, both boys won their starts. Boss is pleased. See you soon."

Her breath caught in her throat at the sound of his voice. She wished he was with her. She opened up the second.

"Great place, Lincoln, need to save up and come for a holiday. See you Tuesday, Kitty Kat."

There was no stopping the tears as they poured down her cheeks. How would she save up if she lost her job? A dark hole started to grow inside her. Part of her was shriveling up and dying. In a desperate attempt to hold herself together, she turned inward, berating her cowardice, telling herself she was useless. *It's my own fault my job is at risk and my assignment got lost. I should have been more careful around Amelia. And if I don't watch it and get my shit together, I'll lose Alex. Probably will anyway because I'm not smart enough, pretty enough or confident enough.*

By the time the bus slid to a standstill at her stop, she was almost choking on her own misery, whimpering and hiccupping as she walked up the street. At the front gate, she sniffed inelegantly and wiped her tears away, determined not to upset her parents. This wasn't their battle, and as much as Alex was supportive, it wasn't his concern either. The answer was somewhere inside her, if only she could find it.

With a bright smile plastered on her face, she joined her parents in the garden for a barbecue tea. She didn't say anything about the incident at Mrs. Waldrop's or the threat to her job. Time enough for that if it happened. But by the time they cleared away the dishes, she was beyond making light conversation and claimed a headache. It was easier to say she was ill than try to explain her mixed-up thoughts and fears. She was afraid to tell her parents she was sick and tired of trying to live.

* * * *

Humiliation and numbing fatigue clutched at her as she dressed, packed her bag and went down to breakfast Tuesday morning.

Her mum frowned at her as she slumped low in her chair. "Tabitha, are you feeling better? Are you well enough to go today, seeing you've been in bed since Sunday evening?" she asked.

"I'm fine, Mum," Tabitha mumbled.

"Then eat up and get a wriggle on, or you'll miss your bus."

Tabitha stared at the bowl of cereal and felt sick. She couldn't face it so she pushed it away. "I'm off, Mum."

"What about breakfast?"

"Not hungry," she shouted, letting the door slam behind her.

Her mother's stunned silence, and disapproval, clung to her all the way to the bus. Tabitha hunched down in her seat, her bag hugged to her chest. She should have been buzzing with energy, for they were finally having a hands-on session with the local animal shelter on Thursday, but she couldn't draw herself out from under the heavy black cloud of misery that had attached itself to her after the first phone call at Mrs. Waldrop's.

Even as she got off the bus outside the college, she hesitated for a moment to conduct a furious debate with herself. Should she go, or cut class and just catch the bus straight home? Could she face the inevitable harassment that was coming? But something strong still hung on inside, and drawing on that, she turned and hurried to the college.

She sensed Amelia behind. She walked faster, but moments later Amelia grabbed her shoulder, halting her forward movement and almost hauling her off her feet.

"Wait up, Fishbait."

Tabitha tried to pull away. "We have nothing to talk about, Amelia. Let me go or we'll be late for class."

"Awww, come on now, Fishbait. I just wanted to ask if the old duck was as mad as hell on Sunday. I bet she sacked ya."

Tabitha ripped herself free of Amelia's clutching fingers. "No, she didn't actually — she knew who to blame."

"Really. Well, well, we'll have to do something about that."

Tabitha struggled with her tears. "Leave me alone, Amelia. Stay away from Mrs. Waldrop's shop."

"Can't make me, Fishbait. I might just pay a visit on Thursday night."

"Why are you doing this, Amelia? What've I ever done to you?"

"Plenty, bitch, and you're gonna pay for it."

Tabitha turned away from her bully and almost ran toward the classroom, with Amelia's strident laughter bouncing off the walls of the corridor, mocking her fear.

She was panting as she slipped into her seat beside Alex.

"You okay, Tabitha?"

She nodded, already withering inside as she lied to Alex by omission, but it was just too humiliating to tell him she was about to lose her job because she couldn't stand up to Amelia. She was terrified he would think she was such a wuss.

It was a complicated lecture looking at infection-control policies and procedures in preparation for their hands-on session on Thursday.

"Okay, guys, there will be an assessment at the end of the day and it is mandatory to pass or you cannot attend the session at the animal sanctuary."

As Kayne packed up the projector, Alex looked at her and

56

grinned.

"Well, what did you think, Tabitha? You should be used to some of that from working at the clinic," he said.

"Not too bad actually. We use most of those policies and procedures at the clinic," she replied.

"Yes, we use some of them at the stables—boss does not like cross infection if one horse gets sick." Alex began stuffing his materials in his bag. "I've promised to take Leo down to pick up his car. I should be back in about an hour. Shall I meet you in the caf?"

Tabitha carefully hid her disappointment, because she had no intention of explaining to Alex why she didn't really want to be alone today. "Yeah, I'll get the table by the window if I can."

"Okay, see you soon."

She watched the two guys leave then finished packing up her stuff. A chair scraped on the floor right behind her, but before she could stand up and escape, Amelia was leaning over her.

"You're gonna get sacked," she whispered in Tabitha's ear.

Tabitha flinched and sat perfectly still, unable to voice a response as she struggled to hold back her tears. *Damn, damn, damn. For God's sake, bugger off, Amelia.*

"You know, don't you? You're gonna get sacked," Amelia said again, dragging the word 'sacked' out to double its length.

Tabitha leaped out of the chair, shot Amelia a glare and ran out of the classroom.

Amelia was right behind her. "You're gonna get sacked," she called after Tabitha as she hurried down the steps to the café.

In the café, she claimed the window table and bought food. Just the smell of it brought on a wave of nausea. Tabitha pushed it aside and opened her lecture notes. She began to read, but the text on the page didn't make sense. She read and reread the same paragraph. It wasn't sinking in. She kept looking up and glancing around the room. Despite the fact that she couldn't see Amelia, she could almost feel the cruel tentacles of her taunts wrapping themselves around her. Digging into her—scattering her mind and scrambling her brain. She hunched down over her books, but immediately berated herself. *What an idiot. Do you think you can hide, disappear because you huddle down? Nobody is going to miss seeing you, fatty. You're too big to hide unless you got a barn.*

She glanced around the café again. No Amelia. Then she saw Dawn and Petra in the opposite corner and at the same moment, she sensed someone was standing behind her.

"You're gonna get sacked, Tubby Tabby," Amelia sang in a droning voice right next to her ear, then waltzed off before Tabitha could reply.

Tabitha just sat there, frozen in her own miserable nightmare. When she finally turned and looked at her tormentor, Amelia just raised her bottle of drink in a mocking salute to her. Tabitha immediately turned away, wishing she hadn't looked in the first place.

"Great, you got food for me," Alex said as he slipped into the seat opposite her and reached for her unopened roll.

Leo plonked himself down in the other spare chair. "Anyone want anything?" he asked.

Tabitha shook her head. "No, I'm all good, thanks, Leo."

As Leo left, Alex leaned forward. "She been giving you shit then?"

Tabitha nodded. "Just the usual."

"Smile, Kitty Kat, just ignore the bitch," Alex urged.

Tabitha gave an insipid smile. "I'm trying, but she makes it hard."

"Yeah, she does, but you have to be tougher," Alex said, then bit into the roll and munched enthusiastically.

While the boys ate, they went through the lecture notes, determined to be ready for the assessment. None of them wanted to miss out on the best part of the course—a hands-on session.

Dawn was the only one who failed and Kayne gave her a chance to sit the assessment again if she came in early on Thursday morning. Leo and Alex both walked Tabitha to the bus and she felt a little mollified by their joint success as she watched them head off to the car park through the rear window of the bus. Thursday was going to be fun.

Chapter Three

She was barely home when her phone started to beep. She looked at the screen and was immediately unsettled because it was a number she didn't recognize. Her nerves prickled along the back of her neck and her hands trembled slightly as she opened the message.

You're gonna get sacked if you come to college on Thursday. We don't want you there. Stay away and I might let you keep your job.

Her breath caught in her throat. Amelia was blackmailing her — her job versus a mandatory fail of the course if she didn't attend the hands-on session. The messages kept coming. Tabitha didn't open them. Nausea roiled in her stomach. She gasped for breath, but her throat clenched against the sobs trying to escape, cutting off the air. Eventually maddened by the noise, she turned the phone off. She claimed she had a headache and went to bed.

Sleep remained elusive as she tossed and turned. Her head throbbed, her throat ached and her eyes burned with tears and tiredness. About two in the morning, she crept into her parents' bedroom and woke her mother.

"Mum, have you got something to help me sleep?"

"I don't think you should be taking sleeping pills, Tabitha. Besides, they're prescribed for me."

"Mum, please. I can't sleep and I have this big session at college tomorrow. Please, just this once."

Her mother sighed. "All right, just this once. On the top shelf in the bathroom. Just take one tablet. I'll wake you on time in the morning."

"Thanks, Mum."

Her mother turned over and cuddled back down as Tabitha crept away.

She took one pill as advised and soon she was feeling drowsy.

* * * *

She was a bit muzzy-headed when her mother woke her, but a shower and breakfast fixed that. Unfortunately there was nothing she could do with the barbed wire twisting around her insides and the clamp tightening its hold on her chest all the way to the campus.

As Tabitha crossed the car park, Amelia sidled up behind her.

"So you turned up, Tubby. Didn't take my advice and stay home. These people really don't want you playing with their animals, dragging that terrible fishy smell around with you. Besides, I don't think there will be room for you in the van—too big a butt," she whispered in Tabitha's ear.

Tabitha felt the words as if they were physical blows. She cringed and dropped her gaze to the ground in an effort to hide the burning redness that flushed her cheeks.

"Shut up, Eckerton," Alex snapped. He shouldered his way past Amelia and held out his hand to Tabitha. "Plenty of room up the back with me," he said, leading the way into the minivan.

"I'm shocked, Alex. How you could possibly do it with the likes of her, and I hear she's got you in a bit of a pickle. How ya gonna sort that one?"

"What pickle's this, mate?" Leo asked, flicking his eyebrows up and down.

"Really, Eckerton, stick a sock in it, will ya? And you can shut your gob and clean your mind out of the gutter, Leo," Alex muttered. He glanced at Tabitha and grinned, but his face flushed a soft pink.

"I'm sorry, Alex," Tabitha murmured.

He shrugged. "No matter, Tabitha. As I said the other day, we're good, right?"

She nodded and squeezed his hand. "Yes, Alex, we're good."

For now.

The subject was dropped and the conversation turned to the day's activities and Tabitha was grateful for that.

The sanctuary took in and cared for all types of animals. The only ones that worried Tabitha were the snakes. As they got off the bus, Amelia skulked around just behind them, snickering to herself and whispering to Petra and Dawn, who had apparently passed the repeat assessment.

Tabitha was on edge and jumpy as Kayne split them up into groups for the practical exercises, and despite their protests he split Amelia and the other two up. He also made sure none of them were in Tabitha's group.

A shelter volunteer was allocated to each group and Tabitha's group began with the dogs and cats. Each student was assigned an animal and had to provide a general health check using a form that needed to be completed. The exercises were easier than Tabitha had expected, as her practical experience at the clinic came to the fore. She had even helped Alex and Leo a couple of times, but she couldn't relax completely because every time Amelia came into earshot, she tittered and whispered.

After lunch it was their turn to do the horses and cows, beginning with mucking out the stables and washing out and disinfecting the milking shed. Amelia and her group came and stood on the other side of the fence, having been allocated to the milking shed.

"Ah, this is where I feel at home," Alex announced loudly, stretching his arms up over his head.

"Well, I don't, you guys, so some help would be good," moaned Leo. "I don't like anything bigger than a large dog, prefer even smaller than that."

"Wuss," yelled Amelia from the yard she was now

cleaning of manure. "At least the smell of horseshit will mask the fishy smell."

"What fishy smell?" Leo asked, then blushed and glanced at Tabitha.

"Blockhead, Leo," Alex grumbled.

"Sorry."

Tabitha shook her head. "Don't sweat it, Leo."

As she began to scoop up the manure in the yards, the sound of water gushing caught her attention. She looked up. The blast of cold water caught her in the face, and even as she gasped and spluttered under the drenching, another wave of fluid flew toward her—this time brown and filled with chunks of manure, dirt and straw. It splattered her from head to toe and caught Leo in the back.

Tabitha closed her mouth, covered her face and lowered her head as she scrambled out of the way of the water.

"Hey, you, bloody watch what you're doing, Eckerton," Alex yelled, already leaping the dividing fence.

Amelia turned the water on him, but he kept charging toward her. Moments later he was grappling with her for control of the hose. She screamed and let go of the hose, backing into the corner of the cowshed, pretending to cry.

"I couldn't hold it. I couldn't hold it still. Raymond turned it on full bore," she shouted.

"Liar," Alex accused, still holding the gushing hose.

"Yeah, bitch, you just ruined my new jeans," Leo yelled, stalking toward her.

Alex handed the hose to his mate and came toward Tabitha where she was standing by the fence just outside the stall.

"Tabitha, hang in there, the volunteer has gone to get some towels," he said and stepped toward her.

She leaned back. "Don't, Alex, I'm all covered in shit."

"I don't care about that. You need a hug more than I need a clean shirt."

She burst into tears and didn't resist when he wrapped his arms around her.

"What the hell is going on here?" Kayne bellowed from by the gate.

"Eckerton drenched Tabitha and me in horseshit. God damn it, that bitch did it on purpose."

Kayne looked at Amelia. She was cringing in the corner, crying.

"I wouldn't think anyone would do it on purpose, Leo," Kayne said.

"I couldn't hold it, Kayne, Raymond turned it on too fast. I didn't mean to wet anyone."

"Liar," Alex yelled, still holding Tabitha in his arms, his lovely yellow tee soaking up the muddy brown liquid manure from her clothes. The volunteer turned up and gave Tabitha, Alex and Leo a couple of towels.

"Alex, I think that's enough," Kayne snapped, his voice icy-cold.

"No, not enough, Kayne, I saw her — she did it on purpose. She wanted to get Tabitha. She's been bullying Tabitha all year and you've just ignored it. Too hard to deal with, is it? You're bloody useless in my view."

"Enough, Alex, or I will have you expelled."

"Well, what about expelling her, she's the troublemaker," Leo growled.

"And that is enough from you too, Leo," Kayne snarled. "Amelia, go out and sit in the garden by the bus and stay there until I come."

Amelia started to howl in earnest.

"Dawn, go with her," Kayne ordered.

The two girls left the stables. Leo threw down the now dried-up hose and stood glaring at their lecturer, a towel wrapped around his shoulders and another around his waist to soak up the water from his clothes. Alex helped Tabitha dry off as much as he could.

The older volunteer who had accompanied them most of the day beckoned to Tabitha. "Lovey, come with me. You can use the staff shower, and I have a spare pair of shorts in my locker and you can have, as a gift, one of our tees. At least you'll be clean."

Tabitha fought back the hiccupping sobs and tried to smile. The volunteer frowned before she glanced over at the lecturer. "I'll see he hears the truth, and I'm going to put a report into the college about that horrendous girl. I overheard her belittling you well before she wet you."

"I know it won't make you feel any better, Tabitha, but I think she has gone too far this time," Alex muttered.

Tabitha nodded and followed the volunteer.

She peeled off her filthy clothes and scrubbed her skin clean with a new cake of soap. She swayed under the streaming water, then suddenly her knees sagged and she slid slowly down the corner of the shower until she hunched on the floor with the hot water rushing over her head. Gigantic sobs clenched at her chest as she struggled to breathe before they choked their way out of her throat. She hugged herself, whimpering and shaking. Her embarrassment and humiliation were complete. This episode would be all over college by next week, maybe all over the town. Her wet tee had been see-through, showing her bra and all her rolls, and her shorts had clung to her bottom half, leaving little to the imagination. But what had devastated her even more was Kayne's apparent determination to quietly push it all under the carpet. She'd seen it before—because like most people he had no idea how to deal with a bully. Despite policies and strategies, no one really knew how to stop the actions that made Tabitha's life such a misery and perhaps many didn't even see it as serious, because everyone in their day was bullied to some extent.

A light knock on the door startled her.

"Are you all right in there, Tabitha?" the volunteer asked.

"Yes, I'm okay. I'll be out soon."

She pushed herself upright using the taps for support, then cautiously got out of the shower and dressed in a stranger's clothes. She immediately felt self-conscious, aware she had no underwear on, but she was grateful the volunteer had brought her a biggish tee so it hid most of her shape.

Alex and Leo were waiting as she came out of the staff area. Alex had, like Leo, obtained a new shirt, so they both looked relatively clean.

"Okay, Kitty Kat?" Alex asked as he put his arm around her shoulders.

She nodded. "I'll live," she said.

"Damn bitch," Leo muttered.

"Come on, they're waiting for us. Apparently the excursion is over for today. Kayne is seething," Alex said.

"He might be, but does he believe us or Amelia?" Tabitha asked.

"To be honest, Tabitha, I think our lecturer is so out of his depth he's in danger of drowning," Alex sniped.

As they walked toward the group, Tabitha cringed. They were all looking at her, but nobody said a word.

"Okay, everyone on the bus," Kayne ordered. "You all right, Tabitha?"

"Not really, but then one usually isn't when one is assaulted," she said quietly.

Kayne frowned. "I think perhaps that's a bit strong, Tabitha. Amelia claims it was an accident."

Tabitha shook her head, tears beginning to roll down her cheeks again. "Whatever," she said.

Alex glared at Kayne as he helped Tabitha climb into the bus. "You need to open your eyes, mate."

Kayne glared back, his face flushing red. "Enough, Alex."

Alex gave him one hard glare and climbed into the bus.

"Leave it, Alex," Tabitha whispered.

"I'm not finished with him yet, and I will not tolerate some little upstart barely two years older than me telling me to shut up when he is so painfully in the wrong."

Tabitha clutched his hand. The emotional storm of this afternoon had sapped her of almost every ounce of energy and she still had to go to work. She didn't dare tell Mrs. Waldrop she wasn't coming at this late stage.

"You sure you're up to working tonight?" Alex asked.

Tabitha nodded. "I have a spare shirt at work and I'll have

time to get some…" She looked down, her face flushing hot. "Some personal items," she eventually muttered.

Alex chuckled at her embarrassment and gave her hand a squeeze.

"Tell you what, I'll come pick you up tonight at nine, okay?" he said close to her ear.

"Thanks, Alex."

* * * *

As they'd earlier agreed, Kayne dropped Tabitha at the shopping center so she could be at work on time.

"I'll get out here too," Amelia announced as Kayne pulled up.

"No, you won't, Amelia. I'm obligated to return you to the college. Tabitha had a special request granted."

"Well, really. I should be allowed to do what I want." Amelia glared at Tabitha. "I am an adult after all."

"Not today, Amelia," Kayne retorted as he put the van in gear with a slight nod goodbye to Tabitha.

Tabitha couldn't resist smiling at Amelia as she pulled the door closed. Alex waved and gave the thumbs up sign to her.

Amelia glared back at her and mouthed through the glass, "You'll be sorry, Tubby."

It was quiet in the shop and Tabitha was pleased. The menial job of dusting gave her time to think over the day's debacle, and the more she did, the angrier she got. By closing she had made her decision.

"I'm going to put in an official complaint, damn it. She can't keep getting away with it," she announced as she slid into the front seat of Alex's car.

He leaned toward her and planted a hard kiss full on her mouth. "That's my Kitty Kat. I'm writing one too," he said.

They adjourned to the dining room when they got home and together they worked on drafts of the two reports. With Alex's help Tabitha documented every incident, beginning with the push down the stairs on the first day. Alex's report focused on the most recent incident, but made mention of the day Jaclyn was hassled.

Tabitha trembled with misgivings as they each emailed their reports to the principal of the college.

"Do you think I've done the right thing, Alex? What if they ignore it, or, worse, what if they reprimand Amelia and she ramps up the bullying? I don't fancy getting bashed."

He hugged her. "You have done the right thing, Kitty Kat. Spoken up. If Amelia gets worse, we'll deal with it, okay?"

She nodded.

He squeezed her tightly. "Now I have to go or I'll never get up in time for work. Promise me you won't fret about it?"

She nodded again. But she did fret as soon as Alex left. Her stomach roiled. She paced her room several times before rereading her report. Fear of the consequences prickled along her skin and sweat dampened her palms. It was too late now she had already sent it. She had to take a stand, for once in her miserable life. And she wasn't alone. She had Alex.

* * * *

Monday morning as she fed the kittens, her phone rang. It was an unknown number. Tabitha chose not to answer it. The phone rang two more times from the same number. Feeling pressured, Tabitha finally gave in and answered it.

"Tabitha, Ms. Forbes here. I have your complaint. As the college principal, I consider it a serious matter. Can you attend a meeting at one p.m. in my office?"

Tabitha nodded. "Yes, Ms. Forbes, I'll be there."

"Good. I intend to get to the bottom of this, you understand."

"Thank you, Ms. Forbes."

"Don't thank me yet, Tabitha, I did not say it would be in your favor."

"I see. Goodbye." Tabitha laid her phone down and picked up one of the mewling kittens. She cuddled it close to her and buried her face in the soft fur. *I should never have put that report in. Maybe they'll kick me out of college. Ms. Forbes was not pleased.*

She put the kitten back in the box and dialed Alex's number.

"Alex, Ms. Forbes rang…"

"I know. She rang me too. I'll be there, Tabitha. You can do this," Alex assured her.

"I'm not so sure. Maybe I should have just kept quiet…"

"No. It's time to bring it out in the open."

"Maybe," she muttered.

"Gotta go, Kitty Kat. See you soon."

After Alex rang off, she sat for a long time in the quiet of the back room, but eventually pulled herself together and went home to change into something respectable for a meeting with the college principal.

* * * *

A savage burn twisted in her gut as she sat in the stiff-backed chairs outside the principal's office. She kept checking her phone as time slid past, and sighed with relief when Alex strode around the corner. Her breath caught in her throat. He was dressed in good pants and a white shirt with a black jacket over the top. He even had a tie on. He was so handsome and looked so much older than he normally looked. Well, that would show Ms. Forbes she wasn't dealing with some kid just out of school.

Alex slipped into the seat beside her and clasped her hand. "Okay, Kitty Kat?"

She shook her head. "Not really."

The door opened and Ms. Forbes appeared. "I'll see you now, Tabitha. Alex, you can wait out here."

"We'd like to come in together, Ms. Forbes," Alex said, already standing and tugging Tabitha up with him.

"No, Alex, I will interview you separately."

He looked down at Tabitha. "Will you be okay?"

She nodded despite feeling cold right through with dread and the terrible feeling this was not going to go well.

She followed the principal into the office and took the seat indicated. In an effort to hide her trembling, she clenched her hands in her lap and waited for Ms. Forbes to speak.

"I have read your report, Tabitha. It levels some harsh criticisms at Amelia Eckerton, the college and your lecturer. I am not pleased to have a bullying situation in my college and I am sorry you feel you've not been provided with a safe environment in which to study."

Tabitha nodded. "It is only the truth, Ms. Forbes."

"I will be speaking to all parties concerned and making some recommendations. This may include mediation."

Her stomach hit rock bottom like a lump of lead. Mediation, with Amelia. That was a laugh, or would be if the thought wasn't so terrifying. *Been there, done that.*

"Ms. Forbes, I don't think mediation will work with Amelia."

"That will not be your decision. Now let's go through your report one point at a time to make sure I have the facts correct."

By the time the principal had finished, Tabitha felt crushed. Not only was the woman determined to put the previous day's incident down to an accident, she was clearly laying the responsibility for dealing with the bullying on Tabitha — she was an adult, after all. Her opinion appeared to be that perhaps Tabitha was just too sensitive and should toughen up. Fighting back tears, she was dismissed. Alex looked up as she entered the corridor. She shook her head. He frowned, but didn't have time to comfort her as Mrs. Forbes summoned him at that moment.

Tabitha slumped into her chair. *This was a mistake. I should have just put up with it.*

Alex was gone for more than half an hour and he emerged from the office with a frown marring his handsome face.

70

"Come on, Tabitha, let's go home," he said, taking her hand and almost towing her behind him as he strode down the corridor. "Aren't going to get any satisfaction here."

* * * *

Monday morning right at nine, Tabitha's phone rang. It was Ms. Forbes.

"Tabitha you're required to attend a mediation meeting in my office this morning at eleven. You can bring a support person with you. Amelia Eckerton will be attending."

A wave of nausea washed over her. Her worst nightmare had come to fruition.

"Tabitha, did you hear me?" Ms. Forbes' voice was sharp and demanding.

"Yes, Ms. Forbes, I heard you. What if I don't have anyone? To support me, that is?"

"In that case you will have to come alone. I'll expect you at eleven."

Tabitha placed the phone on the table with exaggerated care. The blood in her head pounded in her ears, pulverizing her thoughts into an indefinable mass. The trembling started deep inside and spread until it rattled right though her. With her parents at work and Alex away again, she had no one to call on. She would have to face this alone. *Jaclyn. Would Jaclyn come with me?* Her hand hovered over the phone. Was it fair to draw her new friend into this situation? Well, what were friends for? Tabitha picked up the phone and punched in the number.

"Hi."

"Hi, it's Tabitha. How's things?"

"Just finished my assignment."

"Are you happy with it? I know you hate spreadsheets."

Jaclyn giggled. "Yeah, I do, but it has all come out balanced."

"Jaclyn, I have a favor to ask. Would you accompany me to a meeting with Ms. Forbes? Alex and I put a complaint in

71

and now I have to have mediation. No one else is available and I don't want to go alone."

The silence dragged out. Tabitha waited, hope dwindling.

"Jaclyn, please say yes. You won't have to say anything, just hold my hand."

She heard Jaclyn clear her throat. She waited.

When her friend finally started to speak, her voice wavered. "Tabitha, I'm sorry, but I can't. I don't want to get involved. If I do, then Amelia might take it out on me. I'm not strong like you — I couldn't cope with it…I'm really sorry."

Tabitha stood still as a statue, holding the phone to her ear. She wanted to scream at her friend, plead, beg or order her to be there, but at the same time, she understood. She didn't blame Jaclyn. She was afraid too. "That's all right, Jaclyn. I just thought I would ask. I don't want to go alone."

"Isn't there anyone else?"

"No."

"I'm sorry, Tabitha. Let me know how you get on."

"Yeah, I will," Tabitha said and disconnected, knowing she wouldn't bother. Whatever the outcome, this was her battle and she couldn't expect anyone else to fight it for her.

* * * *

Determined not to find herself sitting in the cold corridor right beside her bully, Tabitha deliberately arrived a few minutes late — just in time to see Amelia disappearing into the office.

Moments later she was ushered in and seated at a table opposite Amelia and a man not much older than Amelia with a dark expression shadowing his face. He glared at Tabitha. She cringed down into her seat, daunted by his intimidating presence. Ms. Forbes took a seat along with another man — a smiling one this time. It was overwhelming to be the one and only — the victim.

"Thank you for coming. I've brought Mr. Milburne in,

72

he's the college counselor. I thought he might help us to expedite this issue into a resolution," said Ms. Forbes.

"Look, I don't know what all the fuss is about. Amelia assures me the incident was an accident. I have better things to do," Amelia's companion said.

Ms. Forbes moved her hands in a placating gesture. "Mr. Eckerton, your sister has been accused of bullying, not just the one incident, and it needs to be addressed."

Mr. Milburne then began his obviously prepared spiel on bullying. Tabitha watched his mouth move as he spoke and wondered if he actually believed what he was saying or if he already knew he was wasting precious breath. Ms. Forbes sat there looking justified while Amelia twirled a strand of hair around and around one finger, her eyes glazing over.

When Mr. Milburne finally fell silent, Ms. Forbes read a few points from Tabitha's report. When she'd finished she laid it down on the table. "There are witnesses to some of these incidents, but I would prefer not to involve other students."

Amelia's brother turned in his seat and leaned into Amelia. "Well, Amelia, what've you got to say for yourself? Did you bully her?" he said, pointing at Tabitha.

Amelia shook her head. "Can't call it bullying. I just sling off at her occasionally — she's such a klutz."

Bitch, bitch, bitch. Damn lying bitch.

"Really, Amelia, you know it's cruel and unfair to put other people down." Ms. Forbes sounded scandalized.

Amelia shrugged. "Well, she's such a sook and it's fun getting a reaction. I don't mean any harm."

Tabitha sat paralyzed in her chair. Her breath huffed out of her lungs as if she had been physically punched. Humiliation roared through her, followed quickly by rage. *She doesn't mean any harm? Bullshit.*

Ms. Forbes looked at Tabitha. "Would you like to say something, Tabitha?"

Tabitha looked straight at Amelia. The girl opposite her smirked and raised her eyebrows. The carefully rehearsed words Tabitha had planned to say became jumbled in her head. Her stomach clenched and burned.

"Why do you do it, Amelia?" she finally blurted out.

Amelia shrugged.

"It upsets me. Hurts me. Please leave me alone."

Amelia looked down toward her lap.

"Amelia, you'd better say you're sorry and keep your mouth shut in future," growled her brother.

"Yes, Lloyd," Amelia mumbled.

"In view of your admission, Amelia, to verbally harassing Tabitha, I am going to make this an official warning. You need to treat other people with respect. I want no more of this behavior in my college. Is that clear?"

Amelia nodded.

"Good. I think an apology is in order, then that should be the end of it," Ms. Forbes said.

An apology. That's all. What a God damn waste of time this has been. Tabitha looked from Ms. Forbes to Mr. Milburne. They looked damn smug. They thought they had fixed the problem. She hated them. Nausea bubbled up, driven by rage, impotency and hopelessness. Why couldn't they see a session of mediation was not going to cure the problem?

"Get on with it, Amelia. I don't have all day to waste on your little fiascos," Lloyd snapped.

Amelia looked up at her brother. "Yes, Lloyd," she muttered then turned to Tabitha. "Sorry about hassling you and especially Thursday."

Tabitha stared at the girl in front of her, knowing not one word was sincere.

"Tabitha, are you going to accept?" Ms. Forbes prompted.

Tabitha nodded as she struggled to get the words out of her strangled throat when what she really wanted to do was scream at them, make them see they had achieved nothing. Nothing had changed. With her hands clenched in her lap, Tabitha looked straight at Amelia. "Apology accepted," she said. Every word burned her tongue with indelible mortification as Tabitha completed the circle of lies.

Amelia smirked and Tabitha saw the glint of evil in her eyes and shuddered. Nothing had changed. She stared down at the floor, waiting for the others to leave. They paused at the door.

"Really, Ms. Forbes, I think you should leave these two children to sort their own squabbles out and accept not everyone is going to be friends. Like many others, I have more important things to do than be called down here to sort a petty catfight out." Lloyd's comments were scathing.

Tabitha cowered in the chair. No wonder Amelia had no compassion.

"Mr. Eckerton, I don't appreciate your blasé attitude. It offends me as a human being and an educator."

"You believe and do what you have to, Ms. Forbes. Good day. Move it, Amelia, I have to go back to work after I drop you home."

Tabitha looked up as the door clicked closed.

"Would you like a cup of tea, Tabitha?"

Tabitha nodded. She was still shaking.

As Ms. Forbes placed the cup of steaming liquid on the table and sank into her own chair, she sighed. "Why do I feel so strongly that today I have failed?" she murmured.

Tabitha sipped her tea and stayed silent.

* * * *

An hour later Tabitha arrived at the vet clinic. She was struggling to put one foot in front of the other as a terrible fatigue gripped her body and bitterness roiled in her head at the outcome of the mediation session. Callie was on the phone so she just waved as Tabitha walked through. Tabitha was relieved because she didn't want to make conversation.

She sat for a long time with the kittens, hugging them, stroking them and wetting their fur with her tears. When she finally got home, her mother just frowned when she refused dinner and shut herself away in her room.

75

With Alex again away at a race meeting, she had agreed to work at Mrs. Waldrop's both Saturday and Sunday. Now she wished she hadn't as she had no desire to play the pleasant shop assistant. But in the end Saturday passed agreeably enough and Mrs. Waldrop made no reference to the telephone incident or terminating her employment.

Her mother was watching television in the lounge when Tabitha arrived home.

She looked up. "Jaclyn's going to ring in a minute. She's been trying all day to get in touch. She says you wouldn't answer your phone or respond to her on Facebook." Her mother's tone made her words sound almost like an accusation.

"Mum, I have my phone off at work, and you know I deactivated my Facebook profile ages ago, because of Amelia." Tabitha almost yelled at her mother in frustration. How many times did she have to say these things?

Tabitha had barely turned away from the door when the phone jangled. It sounded shrill in the uneasy silence that hovered through the house. Tabitha picked it up, feeling distinctly like she was handling a cobra with bare hands. The familiar ball of acid filled her stomach and set up a responding ache in her chest.

"Hey, Jaclyn…"

"Don't 'hey' me, Tabitha Cockell. Why haven't you responded to my texts? Did you create a new Facebook profile?"

"No, I didn't. I haven't been on Facebook for ages. You know I deactivated my account and why."

"Well, you have a new profile and you accepted my friend request. Then I see it has pics of you, taken Thursday at the animal shelter, and a whole lot of shit about me." Jaclyn started to sob. "It's so humiliating. Tell me, Tabitha. Tell me you didn't put it up there."

"I didn't put anything on Facebook, Jaclyn. If I have another profile, then it's because someone else created it, Amelia Eckerton being the strongest suspect."

76

"Why would she do that?"

"To hurt me, to hurt our friendship."

"Look, Tabitha, it needs to come down, okay?"

"Fine, Jaclyn. I'll have a look before I go to bed and see what I can do."

"Do something about it. Get Amelia to remove it all. Tabitha, consider our friendship ended," Jaclyn said.

The dial tone rattled in her ear. She sat there with the phone in her hand, paralyzed by the insidious power of Amelia punching through her. There was no way Amelia would take it down.

"Tabitha?"

She shook her head as she quietly put the phone down. "Nothing, Mum."

Her mother popped her head around the door. "You're sure?"

"Yes, Mum."

"Oh, by the way, love, your dad and I will be flying out to Melbourne on Tuesday. Just for the day. My friend Mary passed away and we're going to the funeral."

"Sorry to hear Mary died, Mum. Please pass on my condolences to her children for me."

Her mother nodded.

"Well, I better go organize this stuff for Jaclyn, and get some study done. Don't worry about dinner for me, I had a burger after I left work."

Up in her room, she opened up Facebook on the laptop, reactivated her account and began to search. Moments later a second profile for Tabitha Cockell popped up—a very real-looking, bogus profile. It even had a profile photo of her—one taken at the animal shelter while she was cringing under the blast of shitty water. She felt sick, then alternately hot with rage and cold with dread, for that wasn't the worst of it.

There were the usual cruel comments from Amelia. Of course Amelia would have known she would look for the page when Jaclyn called her out on the content. There were

77

cruel comments about Jaclyn—attributed to Tabitha—and Jaclyn was tagged in photos—compromising photos—that had obviously been Photoshopped. Tabitha didn't want to read them, but couldn't stop herself. The content made her feel sicker and sicker as she scrolled down the page. She'd also been tagged in photos—crudely Photoshopped photos of her head on a nude, fat body. Tears poured down her cheeks. She couldn't untag them when she tried.

Her throat tightened until she could hardly breathe, while her stomach boiled and she fought the urge to vomit. Amelia had posted on the bogus profile as herself and the words cut Tabitha to the bone.

You're a waste of space in the world, Tubby Tabby. Why don't you just kill yourself? Make some room on the planet for real people.

You're so useless, dumb and ugly. Kill yourself, and take that bloody fish smell with you.

Dark clouds of desolation rolled in to swamp her in a cloying black mood of humiliation, hopelessness and wretchedness. She couldn't do this anymore. How could she go out in public knowing so many people would have seen the images on that page? Why? Why? Why did Amelia hate her so much? She wasn't a bad person—just fat and stupid. Well, she supposed at least in Amelia's mind that made her less than human. Tabitha pushed away from the computer, flopped on her bed and curled up into the tightest and smallest ball she could make—a vain effort to be the smallest blight on the world she could be. She stared into space, not seeing her room, the beautiful, clear night with the full moon lighting the sky, or the curtains fluttering in the breeze.

Looming black clouds of pure misery blinded her to everything but her own distress, magnifying her own inadequacies. A stinging flow of self-loathing flooded through her. Not for the first time, she began to think she would be better off dead. At least Amelia would be happy. Her parents might be sad for a while, but then, she was a burden to them as well—expecting monetary support, emotional support and mental support when she couldn't cope. They might miss her, but no one else would. Even Alex would move on quickly, then he could find himself a less troubled girlfriend.

She hugged herself tight while she let the voices argue around and around in her head as she sank deeper and deeper into the pit. Tears poured down her cheeks and soaked into her pillow. *This is what I get for taking a stand.* It was early hours of the morning before she finally slept.

* * * *

She woke with a start at eight and realized her phone was beeping. There was a message from Jaclyn. Tabitha opened it with trepidation.

More stuff has gone up. Horrible, horrible stuff. My cousins saw it and told the parents. Now I'm banned from Facebook. I can't deal with this crap. Consider our friendship over. Don't bother with lunch tomorrow.

Tabitha sighed, sinking deeper under the billowing clouds of despair that crouched over her. She flopped back on the bed, the finality of Jaclyn's edict cutting deep into her soul, draining the last tendrils of resistance from her. With the covers over her head, Tabitha lay in the smothering darkness, wishing she never had to leave, but she was committed to work. Fatigue weighted her body into an unbearable burden. With a slow, uncoordinated flailing of her legs, she shoved the quilt down to the end of the bed. She then lay there, uncovered, for several minutes before kicking her legs and pushing with her arms just enough to lever herself upright on the edge of her bed.

Despite her state, she arrived at the mall early so headed down to the café just past the shop for a coffee. As she walked back toward Mrs. Waldrop's via the back alleyway, she went to compose a text to Alex and realized she'd left her phone at home. Damn, she felt so lost without it. Not that it mattered today really because she never had it on at work anyway. But she missed Alex when he went away for work and just wanted to get in touch.

Without warning she was shoved violently into the wall. As she struggled to regain her footing, she was shoved again. She lost her balance and hit the floor with a thud, cracking her head on the wall. Blackness hovered at the edge of her mind even as she was aware of the scalding coffee soaking through her shirt.

"Oww," she cried as she lifted the shirt away from her skin.

Total darkness engulfed her—not unconsciousness, but confinement in a small space. She moved her legs. Metal containers clanged. Something smacked on top of her head with a clatter. Tabitha reached up and found two broom handles. She pushed them aside and scrambled up. There was a small slash of light glowing by her feet. She guessed she was in the cleaner's closet. She felt for the handle of the door. It wouldn't turn. Someone had locked her in.

She bashed on the door. "Hey, let me out. Somebody, anybody, I'm trapped. Help!" she screamed.

No one came. Frustrated, she grabbed the door handle and twisted it up and down then bashed the door and screamed again. Being off the main thoroughfare, there was little chance of passing customers coming to her rescue, especially this early. It would need one of the tenants or staff to be passing before she would be heard. Mrs. Waldrop would be wondering where she was—she was never late, not once in the two years she had worked there. Tabitha berated herself for forgetting her phone and being caught unaware enough to be shoved in a cupboard. She hadn't seen who pushed her, but guessed it was Amelia.

Periodically she bashed and kicked the door, and screamed until her throat hurt. Sweat poured down her face and trickled between her breasts as she gasped for air in the confined space. She slipped to the floor and sat among the buckets and cleaner's paraphernalia, kicking and pounding on the door in between sustained bouts of screaming for help.

It seemed like forever, but finally she heard the rattle of keys outside the door. She immediately banged on the door.

"I'm opening the door, please wait," a woman's voice replied.

As light and fresh air rushed in, Tabitha stood blinking at the cleaning lady in the doorway.

"Thank you," she said.

"How long have you been in my cupboard?" the woman asked.

Tabitha shook her head. "What's the time?"

"It's almost twelve-thirty."

Dismay flooded her. She had been expected to start at eleven. She was late.

"Thank you again," she said as she stepped past the woman and hurried down the corridor.

Mrs. Waldrop stood behind the counter, her face set in a sharp mask of disapproval and frustration as Tabitha entered the shop.

"And where have you been, young lady? Just look at you, filthy, sweaty and very, very late."

"I'm sorry, Mrs. Waldrop, someone locked me in the cleaner's cupboard. I've just been let out. I'm so sorry."

The older woman's mouth pursed into a thin line. "I understand you have issues with that little vixen, but you were rostered on for eleven, and you've left me in a terrible quandary. I've had to call my niece, Janie, into help."

Tabitha could see Janie hiding in the stockroom. She didn't want any part of Tabitha's dressing-down.

"I'm so sorry, Mrs. Waldrop. I think it was Amelia…"

"That may well be, but I've had more than enough of your bully, Tabitha. I'm sorry, but you might as well go home now. I'll pay your outstanding wages into your account

81

tomorrow. Please don't return. I just can't cope with such pranks."

"Please, Mrs. Waldrop, don't sack me, please."

"I'm sorry, Tabitha, you've been a good employee, but I will not tolerate the company you keep. It disrupts my equilibrium. I do wish you well for the future."

"Please, Mrs. Waldrop."

The older woman shook her head. "Go home, Tabitha."

Stunned by her predicament, she turned and walked out of the shop. She didn't remember finding her way to the bus stop, but she must have for the next thing she was entering her own front door.

She fell into her mother's arms and wailed. "Mum, I lost my job. Amelia got me sacked. She said she would." Her choking tears cut off any other words.

"How the heck did she get you sacked? It must have been something you did. Mrs. Waldrop is no fool," her mother stuttered.

Tabitha pulled away from her, hurt that her mother could even think it might have been something she did.

"Mum, that's not fair. I didn't do anything. First Amelia broke that ornament, then the other day she kept ringing the shop and finally when Mrs. Waldrop answered, she abused her. Mrs. Waldrop warned me she was not going to put up with such things happening. And today Amelia pushed me in the cleaner's cupboard. I was in there for nearly two hours and by the time the cleaner let me out, I was late. Mrs. Waldrop sacked me on the spot."

"Oh dear. This has just gone too far."

"Mum, it went too far a long time ago, but no one takes it seriously."

"Tabitha, that's not true — your dad and I have tried our best."

"I know, Mum, but it's not enough. I can't cope with it anymore. Now I only have a part-time job — I won't have any money and I was saving for my car," she wailed.

"Your father and I will support you until you can find

other work, Tabitha."

"I know, Mum, but that's not the point. I will just become a burden to you. It's so not fair. What did I ever do to Amelia? You tell me, Mum, what did I ever do to deserve this?"

Her mum shook her head. "I don't know, love, but we can work it out."

Tabitha shook her head. "Don't say that, Mum, because it's not true. If it was, then it would have got worked out ages ago, when I was in primary school or high school. Not now, when I'm an adult and in college, for God's sake."

"Tabitha, calm down."

"I can't. Don't you get it yet, Mum? My life is going down the gurgler. My studies, my job, my whole life is shit. I'm shit."

"Tabitha, I will not have you saying such things. That is a terrible thing to say."

"Why, Mum, why, when it's true. I don't know why you even love me." she shouted and ran to her room, slamming the door behind her before she threw herself onto her bed, giving into the sobs she had been desperately trying to keep in check all day.

* * * *

Tabitha forced her eyes open. The house seemed eerily silent. Then she remembered her parents had flown out to Mary's funeral. She was alone. Flooded with despair, she shut her eyes. She couldn't face the world just yet. Maybe not ever.

A small voice in her head taunted her. Round and round on how useless she was. In an attempt to shut it up, she burrowed deeper under the quilt. A desperate need for the toilet drove her out of bed the next time she woke. Her computer hummed at her as she stumbled back to bed. She paused. Walked two steps farther, then returned and slumped in the chair. Misery dragged her down into the depths. She had lost her friend, she had lost her job, nearly failed her last assignment, probably had failed the practical and been brutally humiliated online for the whole world to see. It wouldn't be long before Alex dumped her too — no handsome man like him would want to be burdened by someone like her. Strange though it seemed, she couldn't bring herself to blame Amelia entirely — it was her own fault, for being a stupid, spineless, worthless wuss.

The horror on the screen called her, mocked her and dared her to look again. It hadn't gone away. It was all still there, in startling color and bold black print for all the world to see, her ultimate humiliation — the proof she was a failure, a waste of space. She couldn't even cry this time. But it was time for it to end. She would remove the burden from the lives of those she loved and escape the continuing torment of Amelia Eckerton. Dry-eyed, she opened up her real profile and typed. Her status update was short.

I can't do this anymore. I need peace. I love you, Mum and Dad, and I'm sorry. Goodbye, Alex, thanks for caring about me.

She shut the computer down. Emptiness swamped her and she felt strangely calm. As if in a trance, she walked to her parents' bathroom and opened up the bathroom cabinet. The bottle of pills felt cold and hard in her hand. She slipped the bottle into her pocket. The dryer vent hose proved a bit harder to get, but with a couple of vicious tugs, she finally managed to release it. With the hose hanging on her shoulder, she walked to the kitchen. There weren't as many pills as she would have liked, but she swallowed all of them with half a glass of water.

With the hose and the car keys, she stepped out onto the veranda. With exaggerated care, she locked the front door behind her. The garage was cold and dark with the two cars parked side by side, sleek and shiny. She attached the hose to the exhaust pipe of the family car and taped it with duct tape then crammed the other end in the partly open back window, locked the roller door and the small access door from the inside. When she turned the ignition key she saw, as expected, the car had a full tank of fuel. Her dad was very particular about both his cars.

A strange, disorienting fatigue blanketed her now and she guessed the tablets were taking effect, so she climbed into the back seat and lay down. The gentle vibration from the idling engine was soothing somehow. She drifted. It was hard to focus anymore so she stopped trying. She closed her eyes. No one could hurt her now.

* * * *

Alex glanced repeatedly at the door. Tabitha was late again, and while he waited for her to arrive and for the class to start, Alex opened up Facebook. He was surprised to see a friend request from Tabitha. *Why has she set up a new profile?* He confirmed the request and opened up her new page. He gaped at what confronted him. Waves of nausea rushed over him as he stared at the pornographic photos of Tabitha. He scrolled down the page with trembling fingers and found photos taken at the animal sanctuary — documenting Tabitha's complete humiliation. *What the hell. This isn't Tabitha's page.* The only friends listed were Amelia Eckerton, Jaclyn and himself. He searched 'Friends' and found Tabitha's real profile. It had been reactivated. Alex knew who to blame. He checked over his shoulder. Amelia wasn't there. A damn good thing she hadn't arrived yet or he would have... God knows he would probably have killed her.

A new post popped up in his newsfeed. He gulped as he read.

I can't do this anymore. I need peace. I love you, Mum and Dad, and I'm sorry. Goodbye, Alex, thanks for caring about me.

Each word stabbed at him, sharp darts of ice right into his soul. Her words could only mean one thing. Tabitha

85

was going to kill herself. He checked the time of the post. Five minutes ago. He snatched his phone from the desk and dialed Tabitha's number. It rang and rang then went to voicemail.

"Kitty Kat, if you're there, answer me."

He typed in a text message and sent it.

There was no reply.

He sent another. No reply.

He grabbed Kayne by the arm, dragged him out of his chair and across in front of the screen.

"Does that mean what I think it does?" Alex stabbed the screen. "Well?" He was almost shouting now as Leo and Kayne stared in silence at the status update.

"Crap, Alex, this is bad," Leo said.

Alex already had his keys in his hand. "Let's go. Kayne, call the ambos and the cops — you have her details?" he yelled at the stunned lecturer.

Kayne nodded before opening his student folder.

As the door swung closed, Alex heard Kayne calmly giving Tabitha's home details to the emergency operator. His heart thumped and he felt sick. Bloody Eckerton. He couldn't lose her — he was falling in love with the troubled Tabitha Cockell.

Neck and neck, the two of them thudded down the stairs and out into the car park. Alex threw ten bucks at the attendant and didn't wait for his change as they roared out under the boom gate with barely an inch to spare over the roof of the car. It wasn't far to Tabitha's place and it was after peak hour traffic. Alex clutched the steering wheel in a white-knuckled grip.

"Got to go faster, can't let her die," he muttered over and over.

"If you go any faster, mate, we'll get pulled over or dead quicker than her. Just hold your horses," Leo cautioned him.

Alex concentrated on the road as they hurtled north toward Para Hills. "What if she isn't home, what if she's gone somewhere?" Alex asked. His throat was so closed over in panic he could hardly speak.

"Don't lose it, Alex, we're doing all we can."

Moments later Leo gasped as Alex raced through an intersection, crossing the line just as the lights turned red. He was doing well more then twenty kilometers an hour over the limit, but even then he was nearly turning himself inside out in agony by the time they turned onto Tabitha's street. The ambulance was right behind them, its lights flashing and sirens blaring. Even as he slammed on the brakes, Alex was unbelted and leaping from the car. He raced up the steps and pounded on the front door. He tried the handle. It was locked.

"Damn. Damn. Damn. Tabitha, open up. Tabitha, it's Alex," he shouted. A deadly abandoned feeling buffeted him. He wanted to scream, but he clenched his fists and pounded on the door again. His thuds echoed emptily above the noises behind him. In the moment he stopped pounding on the door, the ambulance siren cut out and a deep silence embraced him. Another sound, a soft purr, caught his attention. A car. " Leo, the garage," Alex yelled.

They reached the door at the same moment, but despite their desperate efforts, the roller door wouldn't lift.

"Tabitha. Tabitha," Alex bellowed as he slammed his fist into the roller door.

Two paramedics appeared around the corner. "All the doors are locked and there are no windows," the blond one said.

"Find something, guys, to jimmy the door. I won't let it end like this. So close. Damn it, Leo, what can we use?"

It was then Alex realized Leo had already gone back to the car. He opened his mouth to yell at his mate, but shut it with a snap when he saw him returning with a wheel wrench in his hand.

"Move over, mate," Leo said, and shoved Alex out of the way so he could ram the wrench under the door just by the latch. Heaving and grunting, Leo forced it down. The latch snapped. Four pairs of hands lifted the door. Noxious fumes engulfed them. Leo went to the driver's door and switched off the engine. The silence was shattering.

Alex wrenched the back passenger door open. "She's here," he yelled.

The paramedics were right there and Alex stood back as they dragged Tabitha from the back seat. She was still and pale, her eyes closed. Alex couldn't see if she was breathing. He hopped from one foot to the other as Tabitha was laid on the lawn in the fresh air.

"Is she... Is she alive?" Alex could barely get the question out.

One of the paramedics looked up. "Hang in there, mate. We've got her." Even as he spoke, the two paramedics had begun to administer resuscitation. Alex paced. Leo sat in a dejected slump on one of the front steps.

It seemed like an interminable wait, but finally the paramedic said quietly, "We have a pulse and she's breathing. We need to get her to hospital right now."

Alex felt helpless as the paramedics lifted Tabitha onto a stretcher and loaded her into the ambulance. She was so still and lifeless. He felt guilty now. He should have done more to protect her. Deep down, though, he suspected any action on his part probably wouldn't have stopped Amelia's abuse or changed Tabitha's reaction to it.

Alex fretted as they followed the ambulance to the hospital and saw her wheeled into the emergency room. He rang Kayne and told him Tabitha was alive, but unconscious. He wanted to do something more, but all they could do now was wait in the starkness of the waiting room. People came and people went, but still there was no news on Tabitha. It was getting dark outside when Alex saw Tabitha's parents hurry to the desk.

"Tabitha Cockell? I'm her mum."

"Come through, Mrs. Cockell. She hasn't been moved to a ward yet."

Alex leaped out of the chair. "Mr. and Mrs. Cockell. We

found her, me and Leo. Can you please let us know how she is, when you can?"

Alex saw the tears in Mrs. Cockell's eyes, but she smiled ever so slightly. Then suddenly Mrs. Cockell engulfed Alex in a huge bear hug of soft breasts and flowery perfume.

"I can never adequately thank either of you for what you've done," she murmured before she pushed away from Alex to include Leo in her statement. "Of course we'll let you know, as soon as we know anything."

She didn't wait for them to respond, but turned away and sailed through the emergency room door with her husband trailing behind.

It was almost an hour before Tabitha's father returned. "Tabitha's still unconscious. They don't expect her to regain consciousness for a while yet. We won't know anything much until then." He looked from one to the other. "But without you young fellas, she would not have survived at all. Lillian and I will be eternally grateful for what you've done today, and...for being Tabitha's friends."

Alex frowned as he shook Aaron Cockell's hand. "I should have done more, Mr. Cockell, I should have. Then it might not have come to this."

Aaron shook his head. He looked incredibly sad. "Lillian and I feel the same... We tried, but it wasn't enough. We feel guilty for failing to protect her, but we didn't know what else to do." His eyes glistened with tears as he fell silent.

A bubble of guilt welled up around them. There was nothing more to say. They all felt the weight of their failure to protect Tabitha.

"I'll wait here, Mr. Cockell, until I know. I love her," Alex almost wailed in his distress.

Tabitha's father shook his head. "Go home, Alex, there is nothing more you can do, I have your home number," he muttered.

"But..."

Alex stopped speaking because Aaron Cockell wasn't

listening, he had already turned away and shuffled back into the emergency room, hunched over as if under an almost unbearable weight.

Chapter Four

The tube in her throat hurt. She wanted to pull it out, but someone held tightly onto her hand. Her head pulsated with a crushing pain that became excruciating when she moved—or tried to open her eyes. Every inch of her body ached. It felt heavy and uncoordinated, like it wasn't hers.

Tabitha heard someone call her name. The voice scratched in her ears and seared through her brain. She thought she recognized it, but she couldn't get her brain to focus. She abandoned her attempt to wake up, and lay still.

"Tabitha, darling. Wake up. Speak to me."

She heard the voice again. It grated through her head, persistent but somehow soothing in its pain. Maybe she wasn't dead after all. Gradually she became aware of others around her. Touching her, pushing and poking her. She tried to pull away, but found it just too hard. So she remained motionless and submitted to whatever ministrations came her way.

"Tabitha, can you hear me?"

A stranger's voice now. She tried to speak, but the tube in her throat stopped her.

"We're going to take the tube out now, Tabitha. Can you hear me?"

This time Tabitha braved the slicing pain and moved her head ever so slightly.

"Good girl."

A moment of scraping pain in her throat, the sensation of choking, and as she gagged slightly, the tube was gone. There was still something protruding from her nostrils, but that didn't hurt.

91

"How about you open your eyes, young lady, so we can see that you're actually awake."

"Can't. It hurts too much," Tabitha croaked.

"Try." The stranger's voice was insistent.

"I'm not dead, am I?" She rasped out the question she already knew the answer to.

"No, Tabitha. Did you really want to be dead?" Again the stranger's voice. This time it was gentle and soothing.

"Yes... No..." She was so confused she stopped speaking. She didn't know the answer to that question right now.

"Open your eyes," the stranger instructed.

Tabitha sensed the voice would not leave her in peace unless she did. She didn't want to. How could she face her parents? To see the censure in their eyes — the censure and the hurt. Her lungs burned and clenched as she struggled with the choking sobs caught in her chest. How could she have done this to her parents? Hot tears pushed their way out from beneath her lids and ran in salty trails down her cheeks.

"Tabitha, darling, open your eyes. Everything is fine, love. Open your eyes, please."

Her mother didn't sound angry. Teary and pleading, but not angry.

As if tearing them from her eyeballs, Tabitha forced her lids up. She turned and looked straight into her mother's face. "I'm sorry, Mum. I'm so sorry."

Tabitha saw the tears pouring down her mother's face, her reddened eyes and pale cheeks. Her mother smiled through the tears as she leaned in to hug her.

"I'm sorry, my darling, for not being there, for not doing more. Your dad and I love you so much and we've let you down..." Her mother's voice was not much more than a whisper.

"I didn't want to hurt you, Mum, but I just couldn't do it anymore. I couldn't make it stop — no one could. You haven't let me down — I've let you down..." Tabitha squeezed her mother's hand as she protested her parents' responsibility.

"No, you haven't. Now, shhhh. Let's just get you better and back home. We'll work it all out, you'll see." Her mum stroked her forehead lightly, brushing stray hair off her face.

Tabitha shook her head. "I don't see how, Mum…" Fresh, hot tears bubbled up. Her nose dribbled. Someone handed her a tissue.

She looked up at the woman standing on the opposite side of the bed—a rotund, middle-aged, gray-haired woman in a neat taupe suit. Her spectacles were thick and round. They made her look like a startled owl.

"Listen to your mother, Tabitha. We can work this out."

"Who're you?" Tabitha asked the woman.

"I'm a psychologist. I'm going to help you and your parents find a solution."

"Really? Well, good luck." Tabitha stared hard at the psychologist. "Lots of people have already tried and failed. Now please, will you all go away? I'm tired and I have a splitting headache." She closed her eyes.

"Tabitha, Dr. Gause is trying to help."

Tabitha heard the pleading in her mother's voice, but she was beyond responding to it.

"It's all right, Lillian. I think Tabitha needs some rest. Tabitha, I'll be back later."

Tabitha didn't respond to either of them. She hid behind her eyelids. She waited. Finally they left, and she was alone. The weight of existence bore down on her as she lay there with her eyes closed long after they'd gone. Nothing had changed. She had failed to escape. Amelia was still out there. Amelia would be waiting. All her failed suicide had done was give Amelia more ammunition and hurt her parents, terribly. She had proven herself a failure—at life and at death.

* * * *

Sometime later Tabitha sensed Alex's presence, but she

93

was afraid to open her eyes. How could she face Alex after what she'd done? She wondered if he viewed her attempt to kill herself as a rejection of his love, the one good thing in her life at the moment. But for how long—especially now?

Tabitha heard him sit on the chair by the bed and felt his weight as he leaned on the blankets and took her hand in his. His skin was warm, the calluses on his palms from working with the horses rubbing her palm.

"Tabitha, I'm here for you," he murmured. He kissed her hand, then sat there in silence for a long moment before he spoke again. "Tabitha, this doesn't change how I feel, please open your eyes and talk to me. I love you."

She hesitated for a short moment then opened her eyes.

Alex smiled. "At last, you're awake. I've been so worried." He leaned in and kissed her lightly.

The touch of his mouth was the sweetest thing she had ever experienced. Tears welled in her eyes. If she had died, she would have never experienced his kisses again. What had she been thinking?

"Don't cry, Tabitha. We'll work this all out. Just promise me you won't do that again."

She shook her head slightly. "I won't, Alex, I promise, but I don't know how to go on, how to face everyone. It was bad enough before."

He leaned in and kissed her again. "Never mind the others, Tabitha, you've got me."

She smiled and nodded, but knew even as she did that Alex's love alone would not be enough. There was something else she needed, and she wasn't even sure what it was.

* * * *

Her sessions with Dr. Gause were excruciating, especially when her parents attended. Their obvious guilt about what had happened made Tabitha squirm. It wasn't their fault, it was hers. At first when Dr. Gause encouraged them to talk, all her mother did was cry. Tabitha came away with more strategies — strategies she knew wouldn't work — and a deep sense of cynicism. Dr. Gause had gone to the Eckerton house and spoken briefly to Amelia and her parents about her role in Tabitha's suicide attempt. Amelia's response to Dr. Gause's concerns had been to laugh and say, *'Tell the princess to toughen up.'* Her parents had dismissed Dr. Gause and completely denied any responsibility on Amelia's part. They didn't even move in the same social circle after all, so why would Amelia concern herself with one such as Tabitha Cockell? As Tabitha's sessions continued, her mother insisted it all stemmed from the ballet concert when both girls had been changed from fairies to other characters because they didn't conform to the ballet teacher's notion of what a ballerina should look like. Tabitha had been deemed too fat and Amelia too tall. Tabitha remembered the all-out bitter confrontation her mother had had with the teacher over it. Tabitha had remained a fairy for the concert, but had never gone back to ballet the next term. Amelia's mother had just shrugged acceptance at the last rehearsal when told of the change to her daughter's role in the concert. In the end, Amelia had been too distraught to take her place on stage and her angry mother had hustled her out of the hall. At the time Tabitha had felt sorry for her.

Despite the fact that nothing could be confirmed in Amelia's absence, Dr. Gause was convinced that her problem with Tabitha had started with the concert. But on further probing, Tabitha soon recalled plenty of instances where Amelia had ranted at her about being spoiled, a mummy's girl and a sook during school events when Amelia had had to participate without parental support. In bitter tones Tabitha had told Dr. Gause how over the years the taunts had become constant and more generic with Amelia rubbishing Tabitha about anything and everything. "I would suggest, Tabitha, that Amelia is jealous of you because you had what she wanted so badly — parental participation."

"But I'm not to blame for that. Shouldn't she be angry at her parents?" Tabitha protested.

Dr. Gause leaned forward and gave a sad smile. "You're not to blame, but you were an easier target than her parents. I've met them and her father is quite intimidating. And her mother? Well, let's just say she's not very maternal."

"That's still not fair," Tabitha wailed.

Dr. Gause closed the file in front of her. "I know, Tabitha, but there are a lot of things in life that are not fair. You have to find the strength within to deal with life's hard lessons. I'm here to help, along with your parents."

* * * *

At last she was released from hospital. Tabitha came home. Nothing had changed. She was still trapped in her own private hell. A hell orchestrated by her nemesis. A nemesis no one knew how to stop. Her parents' care seemed almost suffocating, unquestioningly supportive and protective, and many times Tabitha wanted to scream at them to get out of her face, but she never did. She loved them. They really cared and only wanted to help. She knew they loved her, but all that love could not banish her nightmare. In desperation, she retreated to her room — to her bed. It was safe in bed.

Jaclyn had rung to speak with her, but she'd refused to take her calls. She couldn't bear any link to the outside world, particularly to the college and Amelia. Besides, she felt such a fool — one, for trying to kill herself, and two, for failing. Facing what everyone was thinking but not saying was beyond her coping ability at the moment. She didn't know whether to be angry at Alex for dragging her back to her miserable life or glad that he had saved her from dying. They hadn't discussed it, and with him away at a racing carnival in the country, she hadn't seen him since she'd been discharged from hospital. She knew they would have to have a 'talk' about her suicide attempt, but she wasn't ready just yet. Although she missed him terribly, she was glad she had some time alone to work things out in her head. Most people were sympathetic and wanted to help, but a few seemed uncomfortable with what had happened and stayed away from her and her parents. It all made her feel guilty, but she couldn't bring herself to face the world.

* * * *

Being curled up in her bed, with the wind and rain lashing the window outside, made her feel cocooned and safe. She had successfully avoided almost all human contact for the past week. With the storm, it was unlikely anyone would come to visit, only to be turned away by her long-suffering mother. She could relax. Tabitha knew her hibernation frustrated her mum, but nevertheless she remained, at all times, supportive and sympathetic. It drove Tabitha insane. She didn't know what she wanted from her parents, but their sympathy wasn't it. Perhaps if they had railed, yelled at her or made demands of her, she would have felt better. She didn't know, because having crawled into her hole, she didn't have the strength to find her way out again. All the time, her nemesis loomed huge in her mind. Ever-present, hovering, in the background — yet to be faced.

She opened her eyes to deep blackness. Outside the wind howled and the rain and hail lashed at the window, but it wasn't the sounds of the storm that had woken her. A noise she didn't recognize rose above the commotion of the wild weather — an agonized screech, a snap, a thud and a high-pitched groan. Tabitha sat up with a jerk as a swathe of leaves swept past her window, scratching against the glass and ripping her fly screen from its frame. She leaped from the bed and ran to the window just in time to see the majestic gum that had graced their front garden tumble, in slow motion, onto the garage roof. Tortured sheets of corrugated iron on the roof twisted and screamed and in response the branches snapped and split open to reveal the pink-red wood inside. Wet, gray-green foliage whipped and danced in the turbulence of the wind. The garage groaned under its unexpected burden then with a slow grace collapsed sideways until the weight of the tree rested on the family car and her dad's carefully restored Corvette. Fortunately her mother's car had been parked around the other side of the house.

Her father bellowed. The front door slammed. He appeared from under the veranda, dressed only in his pajamas. The rain drenched him as he stepped down off the second step, and clutching his head with his hands, he stared at the devastation of his garage. Tabitha felt his pain. *Poor Dad.* But then, they were lucky it hadn't been the house. They might have all been killed. It hit her then, with a sudden sharp pain—the meaning of death. How easily it could come, and how permanent it would be. For the first time since her suicide attempt, Tabitha felt glad she had survived.

She pulled on some track pants and a sweatshirt and hurried down the passage. Her dad had just come inside. He was saturated, his distorted features reflecting the devastation she guessed he was feeling. Tabitha suspected tears would be pouring down his cheeks if it weren't for the rain on his face. He didn't resist as her mum pushed him toward the shower.

"Get dry, Aaron. I'll call the State Emergency Service and see if they can come and deal with it. Tabitha, make your dad…no, all of us, a hot chocolate and turn the heater up. It could be a long night."

For the first time in many weeks, Tabitha could empathize with another person's distress. Her poor dad. He loved that car, so carefully restored by his own hand, using what little money he could save from their meager budget.

* * * *

It was beginning to get light by the time the State

Emergency Service volunteers pulled up in a huge truck and a four-wheel drive. Rain still fell, lightly now, but the wind had dropped to almost nothing. It was freezing outside. Tabitha watched through the front window as her father discussed the accident with a tall, heavy-built man in very dirty orange overalls. It was brief after which her father returned to the shelter of the veranda and the man in orange overalls returned to the truck. Curious about what had been decided, Tabitha pulled on her coat and slipped out the front door.

Her father looked down at her as she came to stand silently beside him. "Go inside, Tabitha. It's cold and wet out here and there is nothing you can do."

"What's happening, Dad?" she asked.

Her father looked surprised at her question, and Tabitha almost smiled. He had the right to be shocked, seeing it was the first interest she'd shown in the world since being released from hospital. It felt good to care even just a little about someone else's hurt above her own. *Perhaps there is hope for me yet.*

"They're going to cut the tree up and remove it from the roof. If they can, they'll prop up the garage to get the cars out. If there's too much damage, I'll have to pay for professional demolition and rebuilding."

"The tree is huge, Dad, and some of it's over the house. At least the house is okay and Mum's car's not damaged."

"Don't worry, Tabitha. These guys are fully trained. Apparently they've been out for half the night doing rescue jobs like this. Maybe you and your mum would like to make hot drinks and some food in a while? I bet they're not only cold and wet, but hungry."

Tabitha turned to look as the crunch of heavy boots broke the quiet of the early morning. She watched with interest as ten people in orange overalls advanced up the drive. They had helmets with lights, and two had chainsaws and what looked like green cowboy chaps on, while another couple had poles, huge spotlights and extension cords.

Behind them came two more—one tall and skinny with a cheeky grin, and the other, a woman, small and slight in build. They both wore climbing harnesses. She also carried a pole with a small chainsaw on top and wore green chaps. A little behind the first six were four others carrying two ladders between them. The first team was obviously two more women, one slim and elegant with a tangle of red hair poking out from under her helmet and the other a robust young woman at least a dress size bigger than Tabitha.

She couldn't help staring at these apparitions in orange as they went to work. The small woman scurried up the ladder, secured herself to ropes held by others, and took the small saw on a pole from her partner. He scrambled up behind her. Even as he hooked himself onto the safety ropes, the woman had already started the saw and proceeded to slice through the smaller branches that lay across the roof of the house. He hauled them away from her work area, and after yelling 'below' loudly, he pushed them off the roof.

The roar of chainsaws, the smell of fuel and freshly cut foliage and timber scented the air. A light rain misted the area and blue smoke drifted from the saws as they gouged and sliced through the tree. All those in orange not using the chainsaws or holding ropes steadily moved the severed branches out of the way of the cutters. The tall man who had first spoken to her father watched, occasionally giving orders for adjustments to ropes or which branch should be cut next.

Tabitha stood on the veranda, absolutely absorbed by the industry and teamwork before her. Her gaze returned again and again to the woman on the roof. She and her partner had swapped roles with him cutting branches and she removing them. The house roof was almost cleared of debris. There was a long way to go before they would be finished, and already it was fully light.

"Tabitha, can you help me? I thought the volunteers out there would like some breakfast."

"Sure, Mum."

Half an hour later, Tabitha carried a tray piled high with bacon and egg sandwiches out to the veranda. Her mother followed with hot drinks while her father advised the tall guy that refreshments were available.

Tabitha had barely set the tray down before she was surrounded by people in orange. She straightened up and looked directly into the sparkling blue eyes of the young woman from the roof.

She grinned back at Tabitha. "You guys are great to provide breakfast. Thanks," she said.

"Glad we can help... I didn't know they had women in the SES," Tabitha blurted out.

The young woman laughed. "They couldn't do without us — could you, Jesse?" she asked as she slapped the arm of the tall, skinny young man beside her, wolfing down a sandwich.

"You bet, Mighty Mouse."

Tabitha looked from one to the other. "Mighty Mouse?" she asked.

The young woman laughed again. "It's my nickname, but my real name is Isabella," she said, still chuckling as she pulled off her grimy glove and held out her hand to Tabitha.

Tabitha looked at it for a moment then took the offered hand in a firm grip. "Nice to meet you, Isabella. How many women do you have doing this stuff?"

Isabella emptied her mouth first, then said, "Eight, I think. We all love it, and we get treated equally to the blokes. Are you interested in joining up?"

Tabitha almost cringed away, but at the same time some sort of tug worked inside her. An urge she'd never been aware of before — an urge to do something exciting, like this. "Maybe," she whispered as sudden panic launched inside her at being vulnerable to another person. A stranger.

"Think about it then. Here's the unit phone number, or just come up and I'll show you around. Wednesday night at seven," Isabella said.

Tabitha could barely grip the card in trembling fingers. How had she allowed her guard to drop so easily — to leave her open to ridicule? She began to mentally retreat, to hide her interest before she got rejected. "I don't have any skills. I wouldn't be of any use," she said.

"Don't need skills — probably better that way, then we can teach you the right way to do things. The SES way," Jesse mumbled through the last bite of his second sandwich. "So what's your name anyway?"

"Tabitha Cockell. I'm studying vet nursing at college."

"Hey, that would be useful when we do animal rescues." Tabitha turned to face the woman who spoke. Her red hair tumbled down into an untidy bush as she removed her helmet.

She smiled as she pulled her gloves off and held out her hand. "I'm Louise," she said.

Tabitha took the hand held out in greeting. "You do animal rescue?"

Louise tugged off her other glove and reached for a sandwich. "Sometimes, but mostly storm and flood damage, searches for people and things, and sometimes rescues on cliffs," she said.

"Okay, guys, back to work. Johnno and Eddie, on the chainsaws this time. Tim, you get Big Bertha from the truck. We're going to need her to cut through the trunk." The tall, heavy-built man in charge was already pulling on his gloves and helmet as he issued orders.

After a chorus of several different voices providing thanks for breakfast, the veranda was empty once again. The air almost immediately filled with the smells of oil, working motors and cut timber. You couldn't hear anything much over the roar and scream of the chainsaws, but the crew worked with military precision to demolish the majestic tree that had destroyed the Cockell garage.

An hour later all that was left were piles of branches, cut logs and the huge root ball of the tree, with a hundred waving root arms wrapped in half a ton of red clay soil.

Soon that was also reduced to blocks of timber.

The garage was unsalvageable and would need a professional to clear the rubble before the cars could be retrieved. With that decision made, the tall man instructed the crew to pack up. Like little orange ants, they worked to shut motors down, dismantle lights, lower ladders and return everything to the truck. They looked exhausted, but no one slacked, and within forty minutes there was no sign of any equipment. Some of the crew had already climbed into the truck.

Tabitha saw Isabella and Louise coming toward her. Their overalls were dark orange with rain, and black in places with dirt and grease. Their faces were covered in sawdust and sweat. Both women looked like they had been through a tornado, with their sweaty hair sticking out in all directions, but they didn't seem to care. They looked tired but satisfied.

"Thanks again for the refreshments, Mr. and Mrs. Cockell. It's much appreciated and helped us get through. Tabitha, please think about joining us. You'd enjoy it, I can assure you. Remember, Wednesday night—just rock up," Louise said.

Isabella waggled her finger toward Tabitha. "We will expect you," she said.

"I'll think about it," Tabitha responded quietly.

"Come on, give it a try. We have fun too. Everyone is friendly—we're like a big, crazy, hardworking family," Louise coaxed.

"Maybe," Tabitha muttered, suddenly feeling pushed into a corner. She felt drawn to what she'd seen, but afraid at the same time. Would she—could she—find acceptance in the group? From past experience, she doubted it.

Chapter Five

Seven p.m. Wednesday night came and went. Tabitha moped around the house. She was angry at herself — infuriated for wanting to go and disappointed because she'd been too gutless to take that first step. It had been easier to ignore the calling and stay at home than to face possible rejection. She'd made the choice, but now she moved restlessly, aimlessly around the house, unable to settle in front of the television or her laptop. In vain she tried a book, but threw it aside after a few pages.

"Tabitha, please, will you settle?" her mother said.

"I can't." Tabitha huffed as she launched herself into the same chair for the third time that night.

Her mother laid her knitting in her lap and directed a hard glance at Tabitha. "Then perhaps you should have gone—"

"No... I couldn't." Tabitha twisted the bottom of her tee into a tight roll.

Her mother sighed and returned to her knitting. Her father kept his nose buried in his book—he didn't want to get involved. Tabitha retreated to her room and threw herself on the bed. Gutless, that was what she was, gutless. Now it was too late she wanted that moment back, to reverse her decision. But would she have? Now she would never know.

* * * *

It was just getting dark when Alex pulled into the driveway. Tabitha watched him from her bedroom window, not sure if she wanted to see him. He'd asked her to go out to the movies on Tuesday, but she'd put him off, saying she wasn't up to it yet. He'd urged her to go, making her feel pressured, and he'd seemed a bit frustrated with her when she'd refused. Again she had immediately felt like she had failed some test.

"Tabitha, Alex is here. Shall I send him up?" her mother yelled up the passage.

"Yes, Mum," she yelled back as she remained standing at the window.

A moment later Alex walked through the door and dumped a pile of books and papers on her bed. "From Kayne. He says no rush, when you're ready."

She turned to find Alex right behind her. She stared up at him.

"How're you feeling, Kitty Kat?" he asked.

She smiled. "Okay, I suppose."

He reached out and touched the corner of her mouth with his thumb before he leaned toward her and kissed her lightly on the mouth. "I need you to get better, Tabitha," he said.

"I know, Alex. I just can't seem to get it together," she murmured.

"Tabitha, you have to work this out or she wins—you know that, don't you?"

She nodded. "And if I don't?"

Alex frowned. "That's not an option, Tabitha, you're bigger and better than that."

She shook her head. "I'm not so sure, Alex, not anymore. I've crashed out of the course, lost my job, lost my friend and my dignity, everything."

He took her shoulders in a firm grip. "You have me, Tabitha, doesn't that count for something?"

"For how long, Alex?" she asked.

"Damn it, Tabitha, I'm not going anywhere, I just want to help, but you have to try too."

Tears stung her eyes. "I know, Alex, but I just don't know how."

105

He pulled her hard against his chest. "Baby steps, Kitty Kat, baby steps. Now promise me you will come out with me when I get back, just to the movies or something. He looked down at her with a serious intensity shadowing his face.

She nodded. "I promise."

With Alex gone again, she sank back into a dangerously sad lethargy.

Its grip tightened as the days slid past. She was hardly getting out of bed, let alone leaving the room. Her mum became impatient with her for the first time on Saturday morning as she tried to vacuum around her as she lay slumped on the couch, barely registering to lift her feet as the vacuum zoomed past.

"Come on, Tabitha, please. Make a bit of an effort, love. I know you're hurting and struggling, but we can only do so much. You have to help yourself, just a bit."

She shrugged.

"At least go have a shower," her mum urged.

Knowing she wouldn't get any peace until she did, Tabitha hauled herself off the couch.

"I tell you what, Tabitha, why don't you come to the Plaza with me? We could have lunch, buy some clothes."

"I don't know, Mum, I just don't feel like it."

"Tabitha, I understand you probably don't feel like it, with all that has happened, but you should try. Perhaps you could pretend and you might actually find it's not so bad. I mean, we haven't done anything mother-daughter for ages. If for no other reason, just indulge me. It would make me feel better."

She looked up at her mother, suddenly aware of how uneven her words were, and she realized her mother was fighting back tears.

Oh hell—she was hurting her mum again, differently, but just as bad.

"Okay, Mum, I'll come to the Plaza with you. You're right, we haven't done anything in a while."

She stood under the shower for a long time, just letting the hot water sluice over her body in the hope that it would melt the hard lump of dread that sat inside her chest. She did not want to do this — the thought of the noise, the crowds and the risk of bumping into someone she knew wrapped her heart in a clawed grip. What would people say? Would they mention her suicide attempt, or would they pretend it hadn't happened? It had been a cruel lesson to learn that people just did not know how to cope with the act of suicide, especially when faced with the survivor. And she, the survivor, had no idea how to ease their discomfort.

They had barely gotten in the door, and who should be coming toward them but Madge Turner from the car club.

"Awww, Tabitha, love, it's so good to see you," she cried out as she charged forward, her arms held wide. "Such a terrible time for you all."

Tabitha was enclosed in a tight, sweet-smelling embrace. She stood stock-still, not sure what to say or do.

"I am so glad you're safe, sweetie," she mumbled in Tabitha's ear before pushing her away.

"Madge, nice to see you," Tabitha's mother said.

Tabitha noticed an edge to her tone and realized her mother was struggling too. Was Madge Turner going to say something?

Madge looked them both over. "Lillian, I heard about Aaron's car, just dreadful. He must be devastated. Will you make the car club picnic?"

Tabitha's mother smiled. "We hope to be there, Madge, if the insurance has fixed Aaron's car by then."

"Good, good. Well, glad to see you are all in one piece. Must dash, I have my granddaughter to pick up from childcare. Catch you soon."

They turned and waved as the other woman surged through the crowded foyer and out into the car park.

"Shall we have lunch first, Tabitha?"

Tabitha looked at her mum, taking in her flushed face and tear-bright eyes. It hit her again — she was not the only one suffering in the fallout of her suicide attempt.

They had lunch and bought clothes. They didn't see anyone they knew and in the end Tabitha actually enjoyed the day and it was so good to see her mother smiling again. As they sat at one of the outside tables of the café, drinking cappuccinos and sharing a slice of cake, it began to dawn on Tabitha that she had to get her life back—not the old one, but a new one, and she was the only one who could do anything about it. Her moping was hurting her and those around her. The ones who had supported her—loved her. She couldn't expect them to pander to her endlessly. While her parents would always be there, she wasn't so sure about Alex, and she couldn't bear the thought of driving him away with her misery.

When she got home, she made a list—a long list of small steps to make a new life.

First she rang Alex and they talked for a long time. It cleared the tension in the air between them.

"I'm proud of you, Tabitha. I know it's hard, but I believe in you. I have faith you can overcome this shit time in your life. Remember, Kitty Kat, I'm here supporting you. You're not alone."

"I know you're there for me, Alex, and my parents, but in some ways I'm still on my own. Only I can want it bad enough to make it happen and I'm so scared of failing."

"Kitty Kat, you will only fail if you stop trying, and I'll always help you get back on the horse—so to speak," he said with a chuckle.

Tabitha laughed then. "You're funny, Alex," she said. "But seriously, I am grateful you will be there, I might need some boosting."

The next morning she rang Harriet at the vet clinic and asked if she could come back. Harriet was pleased she was feeling better, and yes, she could have every Wednesday and every second Monday. Tabitha thought about ringing Mrs. Waldrop, but decided against it because she was sure to say no and Tabitha's fragile hold on this new life couldn't quite cope with that refusal. She refused to think about college — that was still too hard to tackle. She debated ringing Jaclyn, but decided that one was also for later.

After she had finished making her calls, she sat on the edge of her bed and fiddled with the business card Isabella had given her. Her fingers twitched as she turned it over and over, the neat blue and orange logo flashing at her like a neon light. Did she or didn't she? Did she or didn't she? Her mind prevaricated back and forth as her emotions went from terror to disappointment and back again, as she dug deep into her soul for just enough courage to take that small step.

* * * *

Wednesday afternoon came and went. Tabitha sat on the couch idly watching a soapie while surreptitiously watching the clock. The hands moved slowly. Six. Six-fifteen. Six-thirty. Her parents stayed silent, but the tension as they waited — and also watched the clock — was palatable in the room. Six-forty-five. Still all three of them stared unseeing at the television. Anxiety made Tabitha's gut tighten. Part of her wanted to stay glued to the spot, but the other part of her wanted to leap up, run to her room, change and go. She wished her parents weren't watching her so closely. It disturbed her that they were so keen for her to do this. She was scared of disappointing them, of another failure. The failure to give it a try at all, or the failure to find acceptance, if she did get involved. Either way, it would be another fail at life and she wasn't sure she was strong enough to put the broken pieces back together again.

In a flash of insight, she realized there was no way she could put them or herself through it all again. At least if she went, they could see she had tried, that she hadn't completely given up on the world. It would be a gift for them. She felt she owed them that much, after all that had happened. Six-fifty-five.

She sprang out of the chair. All three studiously avoided looking at one another. She strode up the passage, changed into track pants and sneakers, snatched up her bag and the keys to her mum's car, and walked with a nonchalant stride down the passage. As she walked across the lounge, she could almost touch the expectant hope that loomed in the room like a tangible object. She paused in the hall, but didn't know what to say, so just stood there for a moment in silence.

"See you when you get home," her mother said softly, casually, like her daughter was just going to the corner store for a snack.

"Yep. Won't be late," Tabitha replied as she slipped out into the cold, clear night air. She stood on the veranda for a moment, her hand still holding the door latch, and breathed deeply. The smell of the cut timber where it lay in piles tantalized her nostrils, and in her mind she reconstructed the scene of that night—the volunteers in orange overalls scuttling back and forth on some mission controlled by invisible paths. Everyone had had a place and a job. Everyone had had support. Everyone had had everyone else.

She let out her breath and watched it frost in the air. It was that bond she wanted, but feared she couldn't have. Then she ran across the veranda, climbed into the car and, without pausing, reversed out of the driveway and roared up the quiet street.

* * * *

The huge shed was lit inside and out. Two large trucks were parked outside. Men and women in orange overalls swarmed over them, unloading equipment, winding cords, repacking boxes. She heard the guttural roar of a chainsaw from somewhere inside the shed. A tall, skinny man was blowing the leaves out of a fenced-off compound and she recognized him as Jesse. She couldn't see the two women,

110

Louise and Isabella. Fear held her frozen in her car, invisible in the dark to those busy nearby. She clenched the keys so tightly that they indented her palm, but still she couldn't bring herself to get out, to walk those few steps. Just a few steps, from an old life to a new one, with so much potential offered and so much fear to be faced.

Her heart convulsed at the tap on the window. Her breath jammed in her chest. She looked around to find Isabella grinning down at her.

"You came," she squealed as she hauled the door open. "Come on then. I'll show you round and introduce you to everyone before PJ does your paperwork."

The choice to run was obliterated in that moment. With integration into the bustle outside inevitable, she allowed herself to be manhandled from the car. Isabella barely gave her time to retrieve her handbag before she dragged her toward the shed. Inside it was cavernous on one side, but divided into smaller areas on the other.

Isabella flung open her locker door. "Here. Leave your bag in my locker. You don't want to carry it around."

Slightly stunned by the locker and change rooms, and the swiftness with which she had found herself on the move, she allowed Isabella to lock her bag up.

"Come meet everyone. Oh, by the way, toilets are over there, and there is water and soft drink in the fridge. They cost a dollar," Isabella said as she waved vaguely toward the back of the locker room, even as she grabbed Tabitha's arm.

Seconds later Tabitha found herself in the middle of the frenzied activity around the trucks. Most of the gear had disappeared, and Louise wielded a pressure hose to clean the vehicle. She waved and continued her task.

"Hey, you came. Good on ya. When you didn't rock up last week, I told Isabella you wouldn't come," Jesse mumbled from behind her.

Tabitha turned and smiled up at him. "I had to think about it," she said.

Jesse laughed. "Weren't scared, were you?"

"Well, sort of. You lot seem to be so skilled. I don't know if I will be any good at it," she replied.

"We'll train you," Jesse replied.

As Isabella and Tabitha moved off, Jesse turned the blower vac back on. In the shed, a group of orange-clad people were counting items and packing them in bags.

"Hey, guys, this is Tabitha. She's going to join the unit," Isabella announced.

As one, they paused and acknowledged her. She saw then that each had their name on their overalls. She felt a sense of relief that she wouldn't have to remember their names straightaway.

"That there is Tim, you met him the other night. He was swinging Big Bertha at your place. Johnno was on the small chainsaw, and Annie you met. The others over there are Phillip, Paul and Isaac."

Tabitha glanced right around the group in an attempt to include everyone in her acknowledgment.

"So what're they doing?" she asked.

"They're checking and repacking the abseiling gear. Each bag must have all the equipment required, like ropes, carabiners, harnesses and stuff, and it must all be in perfect condition so they're ready for immediate use in an emergency."

"Abseiling?" Tabitha's voice was almost a squeak.

"Yep. You'll learn how, eventually. Come on. I'll show you the maintenance area." Isabella began to move off.

Tabitha tried to absorb it all, from servicing chainsaws to the various vehicles and the radio equipment in the ops room.

"I'll never remember all this, Isabella. Maybe this isn't for me."

Isabella smiled. "No one is going to expect you to remember everything or know it all at first. We do train you, you know. Anyway, come and have a chat with PJ. He'll give you all the vital information. If you decide you aren't interested, that's okay, at least you came and had a look."

"It looks pretty amazing, but scary too. I've never done anything like this before."

Isabella looked serious for the first time that night. "Yeah, most of us girls hadn't either, now we wouldn't give it up. Anyway, see what you think when you talk to PJ."

"Oh, I'm pretty interested, Isabella."

Isabella smiled again. "Good, because we'd love to have you onboard. If you want to join, PJ can do your police check and paperwork. Then we can get you kitted out."

"Kitted out?"

"Yep—overalls, boots, a helmet and gloves." Isabella rattled off the list as she indicated her uniform.

"They give you all that?" Tabitha commented, genuinely surprised that they provided a complete uniform.

"Yep," Isabella said.

Reeling under her burden of new knowledge, she followed Isabella into a quiet, roomy office with two desks. An older, balding man sat behind one. Tabitha recognized him as PJ from her house, and behind the other desk sat a much taller, gray-headed man with smiling gray eyes.

"This is PJ. Peter Johnson. He's our recruitment officer. And this is our unit manager, Cameron McGregor. Mac, PJ, this is Tabitha. She's thinking about joining."

Both men smiled.

PJ indicated the chair in front of his desk. "So, you want to join the SES?"

"I think so," Tabitha muttered, suddenly overwhelmed by what she had sort of decided to do.

"So why do you want to join?" PJ asked as he resumed his seat and leaned back in his chair in a nonchalant posture.

Tabitha stared at him for a long moment. She wasn't sure what to say. Why did she want to join? Could she explain to this man what she wasn't sure of herself?

"I… Well… You guys came to our place the other night. It was amazing what you did…"

113

"Chopped the tree down that fell on the garage?" PJ asked.

"Yes…"

PJ leaned forward now, his elbows resting on the desk. "But that's all hard work, Tabitha. In the cold, wet and the wind, sometimes for hours, and not every client goes all out and feeds the crew like your parents did. It's hard work. Surely that doesn't attract you?"

Tabitha's face flushed warm. She looked down for a moment then back at PJ. "Well, it wasn't what you guys did exactly, but how you did it. As a team—all trained, all supporting one another. Working hard, but still able to share a joke and a laugh. It was that teamwork, that closeness. You don't see that very often. It was amazing."

"I see. That bond is all-important in the SES, Tabitha, and you'll only get out what you put in." He sounded serious, even though he continued to smile.

Uncertainty rocketed through her. Could she make a worthwhile contribution considering how weak she was? Would she crumple at the first difficulty? Tabitha couldn't answer that right now, and knew she had to explain just in case she failed, again. She dragged up a hesitant smile. "I know, and I want to, but you see…" She paused and looked from PJ to Isabella and back again.

Cameron looked up from his paperwork. "Isabella, perhaps you should go help Timothy clean the locker room and come back in a while for Tabitha."

Isabella frowned but left the room, shutting the door behind her.

Tabitha was more comfortable with Isabella gone. For now, she wanted her background to be confidential. She didn't think she was really ready to share her suicide attempt with the others just yet. She could always do it one day when she knew them better.

She continued, "I've not been happy with my life for some time now. In fact, I hit rock bottom not long ago—personal stuff—and I want…" She paused here and swallowed hard

114

before she went on, getting up her courage. "I actually tried to kill myself—you see there's this girl who's been bullying me for years. It sort of got on top of me with a few other things. I became convinced I was worthless and useless and that everyone would be better off without me. I couldn't go on living in fear anymore. But after, I realized how much I was loved and how much I would have been missed. I know what I did was selfish, and hurt people around me, but there seemed no way out of the pain. No way to stop the hurt."

Tabitha shifted forward in the seat. "I'm glad I didn't die, but trying to fix my life has been a struggle. I had no direction, I just knew I needed to make a change.

"I saw something the other night with you guys, and I've given it lots of thought. I want that something to be part of my life… I'm not sure how much I have to offer and I don't have any skills."

PJ laughed then. "Skills we can teach, Tabitha. Attitude, we cannot." His expression sobered. "We don't tolerate bullies in this unit either. Your suicide attempt means you have really been struggling with life. Bullying is insidious, vicious. Has she stopped tormenting you since your suicide attempt?"

Tabitha shook her head. "I haven't actually seen her, but her parents refused to let her participate in therapy sessions."

"Do you feel that counseling has helped you?"

Again Tabitha shook her head. "Not really. The counselors have given me lots of strategies, but they probably won't work."

PJ looked serious. "It's disappointing you haven't been able to solve the issue."

Tabitha's heart sank. This is where they said no, and she didn't blame them for not wanting a depressed, suicidal failure in the unit.

"I'm still having counseling and we're working on the bullying, but I really need something in my life to focus on besides my own misfortune. I thought volunteering might help, especially something like the SES that's so outside my past experience. Helping other people is a good thing, isn't it?"

"It is a good thing, Tabitha." PJ glanced at his unit manager.

Cameron McGregor gave an almost imperceptible nod.

"Will this stop me joining?" Tabitha asked.

"No, Tabitha, you can join, but with a couple of provisos. One, if you ever feel so bad again you tell me, and two, you are not allowed to go on jobs that may be very emotionally difficult, like body retrievals. Does that sound fair enough?"

Tabitha nodded.

"Good. I think you'll make a good member, Tabitha. You have a much deeper insight into the painful stuff of life than most people your age. So go home and think about it. Have a look on our website, and I suggest you read our Introduction Pack. If you decide this is really what you want to do, then fill out the form. Bring it with you if you come back next week and I'll do your police check. We can get you kitted out next week and ready to begin training."

He handed her a booklet, a piece of white twine and a couple of brochures.

There was a soft knock on the door and Isabella poked her head around the corner. "All done?" she asked.

Tabitha stood up and walked to the door, unable to stop smiling. She was in. As she followed Isabella out of the office, she held up the twine. "What's this for?"

"Your training begins now, Tabitha," Isabella said in a serious tone, then chuckled as she helped Tabitha open her booklet to the middle pages. "See these knots?" she asked.

Tabitha studied the little diagrams on the page. "Yes," she said, already feeling out of her depth.

"Well, you need to learn them. Learn them so well you can tie them in the dark, and behind your back."

"Tie them behind my back and in the dark? You've got to be kidding," Tabitha exclaimed.

"Nope," Isabella said.

"Before next week?" Tabitha asked, a sense of doom grabbing at her.

"No, silly, but sometime soon. I'll help you."

Eddie poked his head around the door. "You coming, Isabella? We're going down to the Plaza for an exercise."

"Okay. PJ will look after you, Tabitha. Here's my locker key. I'll see you next week," Isabella said, handing over her key.

Tabitha stood at the door, beside PJ, and watched the trucks leave. Everyone looked excited and eager to participate.

"What are they going to do tonight?" she asked.

"They're going to the local shopping center to build a flying fox from the upstairs car park," PJ replied.

"Wow, that sounds like fun," Tabitha said.

PJ smiled down at her. "Oh, they'll have fun, but it is a serious training exercise."

Tabitha stood silently beside this almost stranger. She felt she needed to say more. "PJ, thanks for letting me join, despite my past."

"Your past is just that, Tabitha," he replied.

"I would never do it again," she murmured, shuffling her feet for a moment as she tried to master her emotions. "I know how much I hurt my parents and I scared myself. I didn't really want to die. I just wanted the suffering to stop."

"I wish I could offer an easy solution, young lady, but bullying seems to be one of those things only the perpetrator and the victim can resolve between them. I hope you find what you're looking for here at the SES—confidence, self-esteem and lots to be proud of. With any luck, it might help you with your tormentor."

"Yes, PJ, it just might. The new environment and people will also be good for me."

"I agree. Now go home and give it all some thought," PJ urged.

"Thanks, PJ. I will."

"Okay, so we'll see you next week," he said as she headed for her car.

When Tabitha arrived home she sat in the car, gripping the steering wheel in a tight hold. Her whole body was tingling and buzzing. *Oh my God, I actually did it. I did it.* She gave herself a shake to dispel her sense of incredulity, climbed out of the car and snuck quietly inside.

"So, how did it go?" her mother asked as she passed the half-open door of the lounge.

Tabitha popped her head into the room. Her father carefully closed his book and her mother laid her knitting in her lap. They had been waiting for her return. Probably anxiously.

"Fantastic. I have about twenty knots to learn for Basic Rescue. They gave me a piece of twine to tie them with and I'll get kitted out next week."

"I see. Well, I'm glad you enjoyed it. Do you want a cuppa?" her mother asked.

"No thanks. I'm going to do some homework."

"Goodnight, darling."

"Goodnight, Mum, Dad."

Later, as she cuddled down in her bed, she couldn't stop smiling. She had known from the tone of her mother's voice she had not understood what Tabitha meant, but she had not wanted to explain—to put it into ordinary language—because using the language of the SES made her feel as though she belonged. She didn't want to lose that feeling, for suddenly she could see a light at the end of the tunnel, small and a long way away, but it was there for the first time in a long time, and it was tinged just a little bit orange.

* * * *

She heard Alex pull up on Friday and opened the door before he got out of the car. He bounced up the steps, grabbed her arms and pulled her close to kiss her. She almost melted with the heat his touch generated. She had missed him so much.

"Ah, my beautiful Tabitha. I'm so glad to be back. How ya doing? Okay?" His question seemed casual but Tabitha could see the serious concern in his expression.

She smiled. "I'm doing okay, Alex," she said quietly.

"Good, then let's go to this movie."

Tabitha knew then that Alex was not going to hound her about what had happened, that he was deliberately making an effort to move forward. For this she was grateful, and it made her love him even more.

When they had their tickets, Alex asked, "So, do you want popcorn for the movie?"

"Mmmm, I love popcorn," Tabitha said.

They got a big bucket to share, a drink each, and made their way into the darkened cinema.

As they got settled, Alex turned to her in the semidarkness and said quietly, "Are you going to come back to college?"

She shook her head. "I don't know, Alex. I don't know if I can cope with her right now. Besides, Kayne has arranged for me to do the first half of the semester online. After that, I have to go back or drop out."

"Don't drop out, Tabitha. Don't let her win."

"She already has, Alex. If it wasn't for you and Leo, I would be dead," she muttered through tears that threatened to fall. "And Amelia would have had the ultimate victory."

"Don't worry about it, Tabitha. Let's just watch the movie, there's plenty of time to sort the rest out."

As she settled back in her seat, Alex wrapped his arm around her shoulders and snuggled her close to him for a brief moment before he reached into the popcorn. The rattle of his raid on the bucket of popcorn was drowned out by the beginning of the film. The movie had been promoted on TV as a futuristic adventure and was filled with fantasy creatures, adventure, war and love. Tabitha became so absorbed she forgot, just for a moment, her nemesis and the incredible pain of the last few weeks. Unfortunately it all came flooding back as the lights went up, and she found herself looking warily around the cinema, just in case.

"Come on, Tabitha, time for a burger and fries."

She followed him through the shopping center, still on guard, watching every corner as they passed.

In the McDonald's, Alex guided her to a quiet corner before he went to collect their orders. Moments later he slid in opposite her and handed her a burger.

"So, did you enjoy the movie?" he asked.

"It was great. I loved Ammedian, he is soooo gorgeous." Tabitha closed her eyes for a moment and sighed in appreciation of her hero.

Alex rolled his eyes. "Trust a girl to have a crush on the hero."

Tabitha laughed. "And you didn't think the heroine was beautiful, especially when she swam naked in the pool?"

He stared right back at her, grinned foolishly, then bit into his burger.

While she munched, Tabitha debated whether to tell him that she had decided to join the SES, not quite sure if she was ready to share it with anyone just yet. What if he laughed at her — or worse? He'd said he loved her, but she was reluctant to expose herself by trusting him with her moment of brash bravery. Besides, it wasn't official just yet.

"So, how's your garage and cars?" Alex asked. "Will the insurance pay your dad? I mean, his Corvette was immaculate and so amazeballs."

"Yes, Dad had both cars well insured. Those volunteers in the State Emergency Service were amazing. They had the tree down in no time, and some of them were girls."

"I've been thinking about joining myself. Just haven't got round to it," Alex admitted before he sipped his drink.

"What?" Tabitha nearly choked on her fries. She coughed and spluttered to dislodge the piece of potato.

Alex handed her drink over.

"Yeah, I should do it. So should you, Tabitha," Alex said.

Tabitha looked up at him as she cleared her throat. "Well,

actually, I went and had a look. I have the paperwork to sign up to volunteer with them—Wednesday night."

Alex laid his burger down. He stared at her for a long moment in stunned silence. Tabitha cringed away, suddenly terrified of what he might say.

Then he smiled. "Whoa! And you weren't going to tell me?"

"I thought you might laugh, or think I was big-noting myself…"

His smile faded. He leaned forward in his chair until his nose nearly touched hers. "Now listen here, Miss Tabitha Cockell. I am your boyfriend, right?"

When she didn't reply immediately, he frowned. But she didn't quite know what to say. He had just formalized their relationship without consulting her and without hesitation. She felt a buzz of warmth race through her. Things were indeed okay between them.

"Right?" he asked again, in a tone that demanded an answer.

"Yes, Alex. You're my boyfriend."

He leaned toward her. "Well, boyfriends don't laugh at their girlfriends or put them down. They laugh with each other, support each other and are amazed at what the woman they love has done to help herself through difficult times."

"Are you amazed, Alex?" she asked.

"Yes, Tabitha, I am amazed… Totally blown away. After what you've been through, to have the guts to do that. Wow!" Alex was almost shouting.

"Well, I haven't really done anything yet."

"Yes, you have. You've taken the first step in getting your shit together. A big step," he said and leaned over the table and planted a hard, fast kiss on her mouth. "I think orange will suit you."

Chapter Six

Wednesday night, Tabitha was already out of the door by six-thirty, determined not to be late. She'd been practicing her knots all week and she could tie pretty much all of them, but not behind her back or in the dark just yet.

When she arrived she could see several people busying themselves with brooms and chainsaws in the floodlit compound. She watched for a moment, feeling her stomach churn and a faint tremble inside. Mentally she stiffened her backbone, then she slowly climbed out of the car and stood in the semidarkness, unnoticed, for about ten minutes.

"Hey, Tabitha," Jesse yelled from the door of the shed. "Come on into the crew room and I'll find you a locker."

She was barely in possession of a shiny new metal locker when Louise and Isabella both tapped her on the shoulder.

"You came back. We were afraid you wouldn't," they said in chorus.

"I gave it lots of thought. I want to do this, but I don't know how good I'll be at it."

"You'll do great. We'll see to it," Isabella replied.

"Do I just hand in the forms to PJ?" Tabitha asked.

"Yep. Come on. We'll go with you," Louise said, already heading out of the door.

PJ smiled when she handed him the completed forms. "So you thought about it then, and still wanted to be one of us?"

"Yes, PJ. I want to be one of your crew."

"Do we kit her out tonight, PJ?" Louise asked with barely contained excitement.

"Yes, kit her out, and she can go on the exercise as well," PJ responded, already filing her paperwork.

"Come on, Tabitha, let's get you all set up," Louise said.

The two girls almost dragged her down the passage into another room lined with wall-to-wall shelving. Tabitha had never seen so many pairs of boots and orange overalls in her life.

"Now, what size are you?" asked Isabella.

Tabitha felt that familiar sting of acid in her stomach. She hated having to tell people what size clothes she wore. Shame washed over her and her first instinct was to turn tail and leave.

Without warning, Annie popped out from behind the rack of shelves. "Her bum is smaller than mine, and so are her boobs. I reckon she would be a size or two smaller than me. You don't want them tight… Here, try this on." Annie chucked a pair of bright new overalls at Tabitha. "Do you have a big head?"

"What?" Tabitha exclaimed.

"For your helmet, love," Annie replied with a cheesy smile.

"Oh, okay. I wear a medium-size hat."

Tabitha struggled to get the overalls on. They were tight over her backside.

"Hey, Tabitha, take them off. They're no good," Annie yelled as she disappeared for a moment behind the shelves. "Here. Try these."

Another pair of overalls flew across the room. By now Tabitha was red-faced and flustered as she struggled to extricate herself from the encasing orange material. She wished herself anywhere but here, in this crowded room, with three strangers helping her to find something to fit. This time she slipped the orange overalls up over her hips and easily slid both arms in and buttoned up the studs. She felt comfortable. She looked at Isabella and Annie for confirmation.

"Yep, all good," Annie said, nodding to express her approval even as she reached up to pull down some boots. "Now, boots," she said.

"I'm a size eight," Tabitha stated before she was asked.

"They're not elegant, but they're protective, keep your feet warm and dry mostly. PJ expects them to be kept polished. And to finish off," Louise announced, "all you need is a pair of leather gloves."

Johnno stuck his head around the door. "You lot finished preening? We're about to head out on an exercise. Isabella, you're responsible for Tabitha. Find a seat for the two of you in five forty-five."

"Five forty-five?" Tabitha asked.

"Yeah, the big truck. You'll see the number on the side," Louise said as she took Tabitha's arm and hurried her outside.

The truck seemed huge when you were standing right next to it, and even bigger when you had to climb up the step and haul yourself inside. Tabitha felt self-conscious in her very bright, very clean and very new overalls. Everyone else had stains and dirt on theirs, which signaled their experience and their belonging. She felt very much the newbie. Phillip drove while Eddie rode shotgun in the passenger seat and Tim sat on the other side of tiny Isabella, squeezed in the middle.

"So, Tabitha, have you done anything like this before?" Phillip asked as he drove the truck out onto the road.

"No."

"Well, you might end up being a casualty tonight," Philip said.

"What?" Tabitha squeaked in alarm.

Everyone laughed at her shrill response.

"Don't panic, Tabitha. It just means you will be one of the 'victims' that lie on stretchers and get rescued."

"Oh. What will I have to do?" she asked.

Eddie glanced over his shoulder. "Pretend to be injured. Paul will tell you what injuries, and then you hide. We have to find you, do first aid and get you back to the truck safely. We'll be using the local school grounds," he said.

At the site, Paul took her and Isaac — another newbie of a

couple weeks — aside, and gave them the injuries they had. He then instructed them where to hide. Tabitha climbed the steps slowly to the first-floor balcony and hid in the alcove as directed. Cold sank into her bones as she sat on the concrete slab with her pretend broken leg and nasty gash to her head and waited to be rescued. At first it was very quiet, and she began to wonder if she'd been abandoned, left out here in the cold and dark. Then she heard yelling.

"SES! Can anyone hear me?" Over and over again they called. They were getting closer.

She waited the required time, then yelled out in a weak and quivery voice, "Help me. Please, help me."

Everything went silent. She yelled out again then heard numerous voices in response, but couldn't identify any of them.

"I hear something."

"Up there."

"SES! Can you hear us?"

"Help me," Tabitha croaked out again.

The rumble of boots on the metal stairs was thunderous.

"Hang in there. We're coming," Jesse shouted. A moment later his head appeared around the corner of the balcony.

"Check the area's safe, Jesse," Johnno instructed while they all waited at the top of the stairs.

When Jesse had determined it was safe, they all streamed toward her — Isabella, Jesse, Johnno, Annie, Tim and Louise.

After pretend introductions, Isabella explained she was the first-aider and asked about her injuries. These were suitably treated to make her ready for transport. Tabitha was beginning to enjoy herself as Isabella fussed over her, and she watched the other guys ready an orange plastic stretcher with a blanket and ropes.

Isabella put a helmet on Tabitha's head and safety glasses on her face. "She's ready to be transported, guys," she advised the waiting crew.

The guys brought the stretcher closer.

"Now, Tabitha, we're going to lift you into the stretcher,

cover you with a blanket and rope you in so you don't slip out of the stretcher on the way down the stairs.

"Down the stairs?" Tabitha blurted out. "You're going to carry me down two flights of stairs?"

"Yep," Johnno replied as he grinned down at her. "Never fear, for we are here," he said, his hand on his chest.

"But I'm too heavy for that..." Tabitha protested, ready to jump to her feet.

"Shhh, Tabitha, you're the casualty," Isabella soothed.

"But..."

"No arguing. Besides, Tabitha, they've carried me before and I'm heavier than you," Annie chipped in.

"Yeah, heaps, Annie," Jesse cracked back. "But no more than Phillip or Timmy. Don't you mind, Tabitha. We can manage easily. Just relax and let us do our job."

Tabitha shrugged. "Okay," she said.

With her reluctant agreement, they proceeded to lift her into the stretcher. Isabella explained what was happening as she was wrapped in a blanket and a rope was wound around her then tied securely to the sides of the stretcher. She could hardly move. As she lay there, the six crew members moved into formation around the stretcher.

Johnno called, "Ready. Lift."

Suddenly she was above the ground. Isabella was by her head and she explained each move.

"Forward," Johnno yelled.

Astounded at the ease with which they maneuvered along the balcony, around the corner and down two flights of stairs lugging the stretcher between them, Tabitha lay there surrounded by the group, grinning. This was fun. She felt secure and safe in the mobile stretcher, and her admiration for these people grew even more knowing that they did this for real.

At the bottom of the stairs, they placed her stretcher on the ground and took a quick breather before it was up and off. The huddled group crossed the assembly ground, rounded a building then moved toward the gate at a fast walk. At the truck, they laid the stretcher down, and Paul did a quick check of the knots and trappings before they released her and helped her to stand up. Looking over her shoulder, she saw the other team, led by Eddie, round the corner of another building. They immediately became the subject of some good-natured ribbing, which the second team deflected with a couple of funny retorts. There was no animosity.

Isabella showed her how they packed things up, and where the equipment went in the truck. She stressed that everything had to go back in working order and in the right place, so they were there in an emergency. Tabitha felt exhilarated as she helped push the stretchers back in the trays at the rear of the truck. The combination of cold air, laughter, workmanship and camaraderie was intoxicating.

"Right. Back to the unit. Good job, everyone," Paul said.

After they made everything shipshape in the unit compound, they had a short meeting before being dismissed. As Tabitha went to leave, Eddie tapped her on the shoulder.

"You coming to the pub for a quick drink?" he asked.

"Ummmm…"

"Yeah, come on, Tabitha," Jesse and Isabella urged in unison.

"You gotta celebrate your first night out," Jesse continued.

"Okay."

The bar was small and noisy, as pretty much the whole crew crowded in and ordered drinks. Tabitha stuck to soft drinks because she was driving, but nobody noticed, or cared.

"So, Tabitha, tell us what you do in the real world?" Eddie asked as he opened his beer.

"I'm studying to be a vet nurse, and I work at a vet clinic part-time."

"Wow, busy girl. So, what brings you to us?" Eddie asked.

Tabitha took a sip of her drink then looked around at these new friends. "I was so impressed with what you guys did at our place the other night I wanted to be part of it. You see, I've been a bit unhappy with my life for a while, and I was looking for something to inspire me."

Eddie, Tim and Johnno all started to laugh.

"And we inspired you?" Eddie asked through his chuckling.

Tabitha looked at him and grinned. "Well, the girls did."

Louise, Annie and Isabella giggled.

Louise patted Eddie on the back. "You didn't really think it was you, did you, Ed? Your face ain't pretty enough."

Eddie spluttered into his beer. "Awww, now you've dashed all my illusions of being the unit pinup boy."

"Never mind, mate. You don't need a pretty face to swing Big Bertha," Johnno said as he patted Eddie on the shoulder.

"Yeah, and a good thing too," Eddie muttered.

Everyone laughed and the conversation moved on. Nobody made a move to leave until the clock on the wall chimed midnight and the bartender had begun to clean up behind the bar.

* * * *

She hadn't been on Facebook since her suicide attempt, and only answered or replied to phone calls and texts from people she knew. Her parents were very protective and watchful of her every mood and action. So far there had been nothing from Amelia and no sneering messages from acquaintances about the disgusting photos on the bogus profile. Jaclyn had sent flowers and a card, but she'd heard nothing more from her. She guessed that fledgling friendship was dead.

Alex would call or come by a couple of times a week, and she soon came to rely on his contact and the warm feelings of love and security his support fostered. Only with Alex was she able to let down that perpetual guard she had always surrounded herself with, and it was a lovely relief. He was always interested in what she had done at SES on

Wednesday nights and always encouraging her to get out and about. Although he never pushed her about returning to college, she admitted to herself she was still hiding from the real world, and struggling to accept the reality that she could not hide from forever.

Soon—all too soon—she would have to face the world again. Face her nemesis. She cringed at the thought and wondered if she would ever be ready to cope with that. To some small extent, knowing what motivated Amelia helped her to see that her bully's action were more about Amelia's own problems than Tabitha's inadequacies or appearance. Unfortunately she didn't believe for one second that it would help her face it without crumbling.

She never ever wanted to be so miserable again that she considered suicide an option. Deep down she hadn't really wanted to die, so she accepted how very lucky she was not to have ended up dead. At the time she had been so embroiled in the massive misery she was experiencing she hadn't really thought through the consequences of her actions. She'd just wanted the pain to stop—not necessarily to die. Unfortunately, she had not been able to see any other way through, her vision so clouded with pain, humiliation and powerlessness.

In the past weeks, she'd felt an easing of that powerlessness. Her acceptance within the tight-knit unit of the State Emergency Service and her growing confidence as she mastered new skills were just beginning to melt the lump inside and nurture something else, ultimately much stronger, but at this stage terribly fragile—self-esteem and confidence.

It was strange, but she felt content. As if that tightly wound acid wire that had always lain in her stomach had unwound just a little, easing the sting. But then, she hadn't really been in a position to be bullied by Amelia for a few weeks now, so her new inner strength hadn't been tested.

Last Wednesday PJ had given her a pager, which would advise of call-outs, and that made her feel like she really was one of them. It hadn't gone off yet, but it was with her wherever she went. She had quickly become one of the team at the SES unit and was gaining confidence in doing the required tasks. She could tie all her knots, including behind her back and in the dark, and she had completed her first aid qualifications with the rest of the unit over one weekend. Tabitha laid her books aside and wandered down to the swing at the bottom of the garden. She swung idly back and forth, pondering her future. The sun was setting and the gully breeze was cool on her face. She closed her eyes and made a promise to herself. She would take the next step in her redemption and go back to college after the holidays, face Amelia and cope with the consequences.

Alex arrived about an hour later and plonked a kiss on her mouth.

"How goes it, Kitty Kat?" he asked after he had flopped into the chair beside her. "You're smiling."

She sat up and looked directly at him. "I've decided to go back to college after the holidays. It's time I faced the worst of it," she stated.

"Woo-hoo," he yelled. "Good on you, my girl—so brave, so strong, and that's why I love ya." He leaned over and gave her a lingering kiss.

"I don't feel strong and brave, Alex, just plain scared."

He grinned. "You're allowed to be scared. What do they say, 'feel the fear and do it anyway'? That's what makes you brave."

She laughed then. "Oh, I feel the fear all right," she said.

* * * *

A shrill screech snatched sleep away. She struggled to focus in the dark. A tiny square of light flashed by her bed as the pager demanded a response. Tabitha stared at it. She was afraid to touch it, almost as if it were a poisonous spider. It continued to screech.

"For goodness' sake, Tabitha, shut that thing up. Make up

your mind if you're going or not," her father shouted from her parents' bedroom.

Tabitha snatched the small gadget up and read the message.

Car vs. house. Crew needed.

She scrambled out of bed, rubbed the sleep from her eyes and dragged on her clothes. With the car keys in hand, she slipped out of the front door into the darkness of early morning. In deference to her poor, disturbed parents, she let the car roll out of the driveway then took off toward the unit.

The lights were on and the truck was already out of the shed. She hurried into the crew room to find Eddie, Johnno and Jesse almost dressed in their overalls.

"Hurry up, get your stuff on," Eddie said.

Tabitha dragged her overalls on, then her boots. She only did up a couple of studs, but by the time she'd grabbed her helmet and gloves the others had already left the crew room. As she struggled to hurry, she could hear them loading stuff onto the truck. She fumbled with her laces then grabbed up her gear and raced outside.

"Ready?" Jesse asked.

"Yes," she croaked, her excitement and being more than a little bit scared making it hard to talk.

"Get on board then," Johnno said.

Five minutes later they roared off into the night, the misty rain that had just started falling sprinkling the big windshield. Five forty-five roared up the hills and slid down the inclines, the exhaust brakes grumbling. Tabitha sat next to Jesse. He grinned at her. She grinned back.

"Excited?" he asked.

Tabitha nodded. "I'm a bit nervous too. This is my first call-out and I don't know if I'll be much use."

"Don't worry, Tabitha," Johnno said from the front. "Just do as you're told and stay out of danger. Even inexperienced

131

hands are useful."

They slowed as they entered a narrow suburban street. Eddie put the side running lights on to highlight the numbers on the houses, but halfway down the street they could see police lights flashing. A red sedan was wedged in the front wall of a brick home. The owners were waiting outside in their dressing gowns, and the police hovered around. In the distance, Tabitha heard a dog barking. Two police dogs whined in response as they, and their handlers, set off down the road.

They all stayed in the truck while Eddie went to do a recon of the situation. He wasn't gone long. Apparently the police had finished with the car, so they could begin work. The driver had escaped unhurt and fled into the neighboring properties, but they expected to find him with the dogs and the helicopter hovering overhead.

"Okay, we need the lights, acrow props, ropes and the big tarpaulin. Once we get the roof supported, the tow truck driver will winch the car out. Then we'll put in more props and tarp the hole." Eddie opened the back of the truck and hoisted out a set of spotlights. "At least then the owners will be able to sleep for a few hours," he said as he headed toward the house with an armful of equipment.

"Come on, Tabitha. Help me get these props out of the truck," Jesse instructed as he opened hatches. "And mind, they're heavy."

Glad to know what to do, Tabitha helped slide the heavy metal poles off the truck and carry them to a spot designated by Eddie. They removed eight from the truck, then Jesse handed down the ladder off the roof. It was hard work. Even in the chill of night, Tabitha was sweating. She wanted to take her gloves and helmet off, but they were considered mandatory personal protective equipment. When they'd collected all the equipment, they stood back and waited. As her sweat dried, the damp air shivered across her skin. Eddie and Johnno were deep in discussion on the best way to proceed. Jesse walked around with the camera, taking shots from different angles before he went to join them, but Tabitha stayed where she was, knowing that, as yet, she had nothing to contribute to the discussion, and she didn't want to get in the way or find herself in danger from falling masonry. She couldn't help feeling abandoned and a little out of it as she waited. She knew it was illogical and forced down her instinctive response to being sidelined. It was barely ten minutes before Johnno waved her over.

"Tabitha, this is what we plan to do," Eddie said as he indicated the house. "We'll put props here, here and here to secure the roof. Once it's safe, we need to move the loose bricks from the car and behind it so it can be towed. Okay?"

Tabitha nodded her understanding.

Eddie continued, "What I want you to do is hand us any tools, ropes and equipment we need. We'll shout at you when we need stuff. I also want you to help each of us with holding the acrow props until they're secure. We'll tell you how and when. Okay?"

Tabitha nodded again.

"Then it will be your job to remove the bricks—just far enough to get the car out while we secure things. If we have time, we'll help you. Got all that?"

"Yes, Eddie."

"Good, Tabby. Let's get started."

Tabitha cringed at Eddie's unwitting and casual use of the term 'Tabby'.

"What's the matter, Tabitha?" Jesse asked as they retrieved the first acrow prop.

"Nothing," she replied.

"Bull. Tell me. We don't tolerate silent angst on this team," Jesse said.

Tabitha's face flushed hot. She knew it was red enough for Jesse to see in the glaring light of the spotties.

"I hate being called Tabby—I get teased and called Tubby Tabby all the time by some people. I hate it. That and people singing 'Cockles and Mussels' under their breath when I walk past or calling me Fishbait and holding their noses."

133

"Fair enough. I'll tell Eddie, and we'll have to come up with some other nickname for you. Just remember, Tabitha, nicknames are a form of acceptance, not teasing, in this outfit," Jesse said with a grin.

She smiled back at him even as she struggled to tamp down her anguish. "Sorry for being difficult..."

"Don't fret about it. Here, hold this upright till Eddie gets it adjusted," Jesse instructed as he straightened the prop.

They worked for a good hour to get the roof secure. Then, as the three men finished securing everything, Tabitha began to move bricks. She was grateful for the gloves to protect her hands from the rough edges, and soon she was sweating again. There were a lot of bricks. She still had a few to go when the tow truck pulled up, and moments later Eddie and Jesse were working silently beside her.

With the path clear, the tow truck slowly winched the wedged car out of its tight spot. The car was pretty smashed and parts of the house wall scraped down the sides of the car, ripping the beautiful red paintwork off as it slid past. With the car removed, they added another acrow prop to secure the house and covered the gaping hole with the tarpaulin. As Johnno and Jesse finished off, Eddie and Tabitha loaded all the tools and leftover equipment back into the truck.

"Hop into the truck, Tabitha. Take five. Here's some water. We've finished this task. You did a great job tonight," Eddie said.

The praise from her team leader filled her with a warm, fuzzy feeling. She had done a good job even though her skills were limited. She'd been useful. Now she wished she hadn't made such a silent fuss about Eddie calling her Tabby — the name had always cut her deep each time she heard it, but somehow she should try to be less sensitive. She wasn't quite sure how, but she vowed to work on it. She was smiling when Jesse popped up in front of her with the camera.

"One shot for posterity and the unit website 'cause it's

134

your first call-out," he said, then proceeded to take several shots.

Dawn was just breaking as Tabitha pulled into her driveway. She sat for a while in the pearly light, absorbing the stillness, tired but content. With her first call-out under her belt, she felt she was truly part of the team, and having been told she'd done a good job filled her with pride. The hard shell she protected herself with and the coil of stinging fear that was her constant companion began to soften around the edges. Just a little.

She could hardly wait to tell Alex about her first call-out. He was almost as excited as she was and full of praise when she rang him later in the morning.

"I'm even a bit jealous, sounds like a real hoot," he said.

"It was. Anyway, you could join, Alex."

"Maybe later, Tabitha. The SES is your thing right now."

"But—"

He cut her protest off. "No, Tabitha, I think you need to establish yourself as part of the crew. It'll be good for you."

She thought about it after he hung up and knew deep down that he was probably right. If he came along, she would immediately have a crutch and perhaps even a barrier to developing new relationships within the unit. It was a bit disappointing, but this was her chance to stand on her own, and she was happy Alex recognized that too.

* * * *

The following Wednesday night, Tabitha was fired up. She got there early and helped load extra gear into the trucks. Immediately after parade, they headed out for training drills. When they pulled up at the local shopping center, she was surprised, but there was no time to ponder as they began to unload the makings of a winch and a tripod, which allowed people to abseil.

She began to feel uneasy. Surely they weren't going to expect her to abseil, seeing as he was so new. A sinking

135

feeling gripped her as she looked over the railing at the long drop to the ramp below.

"So, you going over, Tabitha?" Louise asked.

Tabitha shook her head. "I don't think so. I'm petrified of heights."

"It's perfectly safe, you know, and such a buzz. But if you don't want to, that's okay. Nobody forces anyone to do anything here, especially if you don't feel safe," Louise said.

Tabitha's insides quaked. She shook her head again. "I don't think so," she said.

"It's good to face your fears, Tabitha. Give it a go. We'll be right beside you," Isabella cajoled as she began strapping herself into a harness.

"Well, you won't have a harness big enough…"

"Oh, yes, we do. Go on. Give it a go," Annie urged as she dangled a purple and blue harness in front of Tabitha's nose. "Probably scare the heck out of you, but you'll regret it if you don't do it. It makes you feel awesome when you do it for the first time. Doesn't crush the fear, but brings it under your control."

Tabitha looked from one to the other. These women had become her friends over the last weeks, even inviting her to a barbecue on Saturday. Suddenly she didn't want to let these new friends down—or herself, she reluctantly admitted.

"Look, you don't have to, Tabitha. Maybe next time," Annie said.

Her stomach clenched and her hands trembled as she reached out and took the harness from Annie. "No, I'll give it a go. I won't be any less scared next time," she said with a nervous chuckle.

"Good on ya, Pipi."

She looked across at Jesse. He grinned then popped his face behind the camera he held. "Told ya we would find a nick for you. Now smile—say cheese."

"Pipi?" Louise asked after Jesse finished taking photos,

her tone slightly derisive.

"Yeah, Pipi—you know, cockles you use for bait."

"Or eat," chipped in Eddie.

"But Pipi? Why not Tabby?" Isabella asked.

"Because she hates it," Jesse yelled back.

Isabella frowned. "Really, Tabitha? You never said when I called you 'Tabby' the other night."

"I know. I didn't want to hurt your feelings."

"Why don't you like it?" Annie asked.

"Kids at school used to call me Tubby Tabby—one still does...and Fishbait."

"What little arseholes. No worries then—Pipi it is," Isabella said.

Louise and Annie made sure Tabitha was strapped tight in her harness and adorned with all the safety gear before they helped her clamber over the railing surrounding the drop to the ramp. Tabitha struggled to get herself over, and when she did, she found herself standing on a very narrow ledge of concrete above a great, yawning, empty space. She clung to the bars as her stomach somersaulted then went into hiding. Time stood still while she struggled to breathe, and her fingers clamped so tightly on the steel rails she thought they would leave an impression in the metal.

"Okay, you're all secure. Now lean back and sit in the harness. You have to trust it," Isabella instructed.

Tabitha shook her head. "I can't. Oh my God, why did I agree to this?" she wailed as she looked over her shoulder into the empty space.

"Lean back, Tabitha," Isabella said.

"I can't do this. Can I get back over the fence?"

"No, it's too late for that, Pipi, but we're right here," Jesse called as he dropped over the rail fence and perched on the ledge beside her. "Now copy me. Sit back and let the harness take your weight, hold the rope by your hip, plant your feet firmly."

She copied Jesse.

"How do you feel, Pipi?"

137

"Scared."

"Yeah sure, but what about the harness? Do you feel secure in it?"

Her first reaction to Jesse's question was 'have you gone mad — I'm hanging over a huge open space with nothing to hold me but a flimsy webbing harness, a couple of carabiners and a rope?', but when she calmed herself a moment, she had to admit she felt secure.

"I suppose so," she muttered.

"Now let go of the rails, Tabitha," Eddie instructed. He was standing on the other side of the rails, right in front of her face.

She continued to hold on to the metal rods for dear life.

"Tabitha, let go of the rails." Eddie said it slowly and purposefully, in a voice meant to be obeyed.

She stared into Eddie's eyes.

"Let go," he said. "We won't let you fall."

Slowly she eased her grip on the metal railing and took the rope in her right hand. Jesse guided it to the correct position by her hip.

"Now, move your feet one at a time, downward. Keep leaning back into the harness," Eddie said.

And she was doing it. Her panic eased as she concentrated. The harness held. She controlled her descent with her right hand, one step at a time.

"Go, Tabitha," Isabella yelled.

Tabitha felt pretty chuffed. She could do this. Suddenly her foot was dangling, finding only empty air. Panic ripped through her. She tried to cry out, but all she could manage was a squeak. She tightened her hold on the rope and looked at Jesse.

"Don't fret, Pipi — you just need to turn yourself upside down," Jesse informed her with a cheeky grin.

Tabitha glared back at him. "What!"

"Seriously, Pipi. Just copy me. Okay, keep your feet steady, release the rope a bit at a time until your head is lower than your feet, then walk slowly in under the lip."

Too scared to do anything else, she followed Jesse's instructions. Moments later she was hanging upside down on the roof of the freight doorway like a terrified orange bat.

"Now slowly bring your feet down. Make sure you have enough headroom, you don't want a concussion."

With a shuffle and a wriggle, she slowly righted herself to find she was hanging suspended in a wide-open space. No wall in front, no ledges or handholds, only the concrete driveway, many feet below.

"Okay, slowly let yourself down. Louise is there to help you," Jesse said.

Her feet had barely touched the ground when Louise helped her stand upright. Tabitha unclipped the carabiner and stared, speechless, up to where she had come from. Jesse slid down beside her with experienced gracefulness.

"So, Pipi?"

She turned to Jesse. "Oh my God. Oh my God. I did it. I… abseiled. Oh my God. I want to do that again."

Jesse and Louise both laughed, and she could hear a faint echo of that laughter high above her.

She hurried back up to the roof of the above ground car park and lined up with the others.

There was no way to explain how she felt—free, empowered, shaky, exhilarated—all that and more. An icy thought trickled through her—if she had died that day, she wouldn't have been able to experience this. She made herself a promise right then. She was never going to go back there again. Damn Amelia and all her shit. If she could conquer her fear of heights by abseiling, she could conquer her fear of her bully. She would face her down and banish her brutality for good because she wasn't having her life messed with anymore. But even as she vowed to stand up to her bully, Tabitha felt the familiar burn of acid fear in her stomach. Making a promise was easy—making it a reality was an entirely different thing. But tonight had taught her something terribly important—she was brave and she could look fear in the face and do it anyway. She would look Amelia in the face and tell her to bugger off.

Tabitha was absolutely buzzing as they walked over to the pub that night. She had gone over the wall three times. By the third time, she'd felt like a pro. Next week Eddie and Isabella were going to teach her how to use a chainsaw, but before that was Isaac's barbecue.

"Drinks are on us tonight, to celebrate your achievement, Tabitha," Louise and Annie chorused.

Moments later Louise handed her a lemon squash then raised her own glass. "Here's to our newest crew member — the brave and intrepid Pipi."

They clinked glasses and drank. Tabitha looked around at her new friends and knew she had found a safe haven from which to build her new life.

* * * *

Isabella, Louise, Annie and Tabitha had agreed to carpool to Isaac's party. Isabella didn't drink at all so she was designated driver. Tabitha didn't drink much, and never when she was driving, so it would be a nice treat to have a couple of drinks at the party.

The meat was sizzling on the grill by the time they arrived, and Isaac had a selection of tunes pumping out of his sound system. Isaac was a keen gardener and the setting was almost tropical with lanterns lighting the shadows in the lush greenery.

"Welcome to my place, girls. The drinks are on ice in the Esky over there, nibbles on the table in the corner. I've put a couple of patio heaters on, so it'll get warmer in a minute. Pull up a chair."

They settled in to music, chatter and the delicious aroma of cooking food. Tabitha felt the best she'd felt for a long time. She felt safe and accepted. A small chill ran through her — what if she told them she had tried to commit suicide and why? Would they still think the same about her, still welcome her into their circle? Or would they be scared away like Jaclyn? She could never imagine any of them allowing themselves to be bullied.

"A dollar for them, Tabitha?" Annie asked, holding out a coin.

Startled, Tabitha looked up, suddenly aware that she had been staring into space and not participating in the conversation.

"Probably aren't worth a dollar," she quipped.

"Well, out with it."

Tabitha shrugged. "I was just thinking how much I was enjoying tonight, the company and all…"

"It's not like this out therein the real world, is it?"

She looked into Annie's slate-gray eyes and noticed, for the first time, shadows lurking in the usually sparkling depths. Funny, she'd never noticed them before. Annie was a bouncy, bubbly person, always with a joke on her lips and a caring hand to share. A strong, independent young woman whom Tabitha admired immensely.

"Surely you have other friends and have done stuff like this?" Isabella asked, obviously oblivious to the double meaning exchanged between Annie and Tabitha.

"Well, not really, Isabella. Mostly I got teased and bullied at school because I'm overweight, and the bullying has continued into college, with one of the worst offenders in my lectures. It really gets me down…"

"That's bad," Isabella declared.

"Yeah, but pretty normal," Annie said sadly. "I got the same in my last year of high school. I thought about suicide."

Tabitha's breath caught in her throat. *Annie thought of suicide. Annie was bullied. My God, I never would have thought it could happen to someone like her.* With a sudden rush, Tabitha felt a light of understanding illuminate her mind. It could happen to anyone, not just her.

"Annie! You poor thing. But you never said anything in the last three years since we've been friends," Isabella said

141

softly.

"No, I was afraid you would think less of me, or treat me differently, if I admitted that I'd once been suicidal."

Both Louise and Isabella leaned forward to embrace Annie. "Of course we wouldn't have, but I don't know how people can be so cruel," Louise exclaimed.

"Easily," Tabitha said softly.

Isabella turned a probing look on Tabitha then held out her spare arm. "You too? Come on, girls — we need a group hug."

Just before Tabitha was enclosed in the warmth of the four-girl hug, she said softly, "I almost succeeded with my suicide. It really hurt my parents and hasn't solved anything. I still have to face her and I don't know how."

They hugged in silence.

As they pulled back Annie gave her a hard, direct look. "You have to face her, Tabitha. You have to call her bluff, refute her taunts. You know no one else can do this for you, love. You have to stand strong and tell her no. I know it's scary."

Tabitha nodded. "I've decided to return to college after the holidays to finish my course and I'm petrified, you know, about her, and what others think. Nobody is comfortable around a suicide survivor."

Annie grimaced. "I know it's gonna be hard, Tabitha, but really, their discomfort is their problem. Whatever a bully says is really worthless words — a reflection on them as a human being, not you. Their taunts are lies. The thing is, you have to believe that inside yourself. You have to believe in yourself, assess all your good points — and in your case, Tabitha, there are plenty."

All the others nodded. "Definitely," they chorused. "Heaps and heaps."

Annie nodded. "Think about it, Tabitha. We'll help if you're short of positive traits to count."

Tabitha chuckled. "I might just need that help, guys. I struggle seeing the good in me."

"Well, you damn well shouldn't. Now just promise us one thing, Tabitha, if you ever feel like that again, you will talk to us first. Do you hear me? Promise." Isabella's usually lilting voice was sharp and insistent.

Tabitha pulled free of their embrace. "I hope to never feel like that again, but if I do, I promise I will talk to you."

"Okay, you lot, enough of the female bonding stuff. The food is ready," Isaac announced.

Nothing more was said, but Tabitha felt closer to the girls, particularly Annie. She felt safer having told them herself, and they hadn't rejected her. As she'd become more entrenched in the group, she'd been so scared of being exposed unexpectedly. Although PJ and Cameron had promised it would remain confidential, she hadn't wanted it to slip out and surprise the others.

Chapter Seven

It was late by the time she woke, and her mother was already tidying the kitchen. She grabbed a bowl of cereal and parked herself at the breakfast bar.

"You were late last night," her mother said.

"Mmmmm," Tabitha mumbled through a mouthful.

"Did you enjoy the party?"

"Absolutely, Mum. I'm enjoying everything about the SES."

"But…"

"No buts, Mum. I'm going to learn how to use the chainsaws next week."

"Jaclyn rang."

"Really? She made it clear she no longer wanted to be friends because of the Facebook thing. Don't know why she bothered."

Her mother laid down the dishcloth and looked at her. "But you could have been great friends, you seemed to have such a lot in common."

"That's just it, Mum — we have. It just hurt so much when she wouldn't believe me about Facebook. And now, no one knows what to say to the girl who tried to kill herself, including Jaclyn. Everyone else is too…I don't know… scared, embarrassed. Who knows?" Tabitha shrugged.

"Well, you could try to patch things up…"

"Maybe, Mum, I'll see. For now I need positive, supportive friends and I've found that elsewhere."

"But you shouldn't burn bridges, Tabitha."

She smiled at her mother's frown. "Look, Mum, I know I've got a long way to go. I still haven't gone back to college or faced Amelia, but you know what? After these last few weeks, I feel different. Stronger. Yes, I tried to kill myself, but I didn't," she said softly as she approached her mum.

Her mum had tears in her eyes as Tabitha hugged her.

"I'm sorry I hurt you so much, and I will regret that all my life, but now I have a second chance and I'm going to make the most of it. Please don't cry."

Her mother hugged her back with a fierceness born of pain, anguish, love and hope. "I am so glad you have a second chance, my dear. I love you so much. I don't think I could have coped if you had succeeded in your attempt."

"I didn't and now we have to move on. Maybe I'll think about Jaclyn, okay?"

"But, Tabitha, it's almost as hard coping seeing you struggle every day with your life, that girl and her abuse, and not being able to protect you."

"You can't protect me. I must learn to protect myself. I have to find it in me to stand up to her. I'm going back to college after the holidays."

"Are you sure?"

"No matter how scared I am, I must."

* * * *

Despite the enjoyment of the intervening weeks, the morning she had dreaded finally came. She felt tense, restless and scared. Her stomach rebelled when she tried to put food into it. Her mother watched her with a tight, frozen expression of worry that deepened the wrinkles just beginning to form around her mouth and in the corners of her eyes.

"I'll be all right, Mum. Please don't stress."

"Are you sure, love?"

Tabitha shook her head. "I have to do this, Mum. I want my life back, and the only way I can do that is to face her down and win. I promise I won't try to harm myself again. I really promise."

145

Her mother grabbed her in a tight hug. "I love you so much—we love you, your dad and I, and we would do anything to protect you, but I know you're right. Only you can stand up to that monstrous child. If you're not brave enough, we will understand, just please don't try to kill yourself again, I couldn't bear to go through all that again."

"I promise you won't have to. No matter how hard it gets, I don't want to die."

Despite her show of bravado and internal determination to go back to college and complete her course, she felt sick inside. Everyone knew she had tried to kill herself and failed. It was humiliating. She rehearsed scenarios in her head, how to respond and ways to answer questions. It wasn't just Amelia, it was everyone.

Alex arrived to pick her up and now there was no turning back. She sat hunched in the front seat all the way.

When he had parked the car, he turned to her. "You sure about this, Tabitha? It's not too late to pike, you know."

She shook her head. "No, Alex, I have to do this."

He grinned. "Okay, let's do it."

He held her hand all the way to class and Tabitha savored the warm, tight grip and the strength she could draw from it.

They were the first to arrive. She sat beside him, tense and nervous. She was cold. An inner frozen paralysis, sparked by her fear of the unknown. Her greatest concern was how Amelia would react to her return.

"Hey, you're back. Great stuff, Tabitha. You're looking good," Leo said as he entered the room.

"Thanks, Leo. It's good to be back—well, maybe. We'll see."

"She'd better not start," Leo grumbled.

"No, Leo, this is something I have to manage myself."

He nodded. He understood too.

"Are you okay?" Alex whispered.

"I'm terrified," she muttered and gripped his hand, hard. He squeezed back.

The door crashed again and Amelia, Dawn and Petra barged into the room.

Amelia brushed past Tabitha's chair. "Back from the dead, I see. Couldn't even do that properly, could you?" she taunted.

Tabitha flinched at the contempt in her tone, but refused to respond. She opened her textbook and waited for the lecture to start, seething inside at Amelia's snipe. This nasty piece of work obviously didn't feel any remorse or guilt that she had been the cause of Tabitha's suicide attempt. Tabitha struggled to push it aside because it dug deep, with sharp claws, tearing her to shreds inside. It was also obvious that nothing had changed.

Alex turned then to the three girls. "Shut up, Eckerton. Haven't you done enough already?"

Amelia just poked her tongue out at him and laughed.

"Try to ignore it, Tabitha," he whispered in her ear.

Tabitha shuffled her things on the desk. "I'm trying," she muttered.

After class, Amelia waited at the top of the steps. Tabitha cringed inside even though she had Alex for company.

"What's that smell? Oh yes, it's Fishbait. Such a blight on the world." Amelia's voice carried across the hallway.

Her heart was thumping so hard she thought it would jump out of her chest and her stomach clenched into painfully tight strips of barbed wire. She was trembling, but determined to stand up to Amelia for the first time in her life. Tabitha steeled herself and looked straight at her tormentor. "Enough already, Amelia," she said quietly and calmly.

"Awww, the cockle speaks. Well, Tubby Tabby, it's never enough. You're just taking up space—fat, dumb trailer trash. What did you come back for?"

"So you think I'm fat and dumb and trailer trash? Big deal." Tabitha parroted Amelia's words to her face, calmly, before she turned on her heel and started down the steps.

"Ahhh, finally you get it, Fishbait. Finally!" Amelia

shouted.

"Whatever, Amelia," Tabitha muttered loudly, and waved a dismissive hand in the air and kept going, one measured step at time. She was shaking.

Alex took her arm and she was grateful for the comfort. Everything was silent on the landing. No more insults came her way, and she didn't hear footsteps on the stairs behind them.

"You don't really believe that, do you, Tabitha, really? You don't have to agree with her," Alex muttered as he pulled her around to face him when they reached the bottom of the flight.

Tabitha took one look at Alex's expression and giggles bubbled up. "No, silly. It was just a technique I learned from a friend. It's called fogging. I parrot whatever she says about me to her face and it's supposed to take the power out of her insults."

"And did it?" Alex asked.

Tabitha thought about it for a moment then shook her head. "I don't know. Her words still stung, but she did shut up, and I sort of feel—I don't know—like I've finally risen above her taunts. Actually, it feels okay to have answered her back."

"Well then, that's okay," Alex responded as he took her hand in his and proceeded to walk her to the bus stop even though it was out of his way to the car park. He waited until the bus was in sight. He gave her a lingering kiss as it pulled up. "Here's your bus. I'll see you Thursday, and are we on for some bowling on Friday night?"

"I'd like that," she said as she stepped up into the bus.

Her knees barely held her upright as she walked slowly to the back of the bus. She sank into the seat, every inch of her trembling. She took a couple of deep breaths and clutched the edge of the seat with a tight grip. Waves of nausea washed over her, but at the same time, she felt the tiny nugget of courage that had been born inside her when she joined the SES spark and begin to grow. She'd done it.

Really done it. Of course she knew it wasn't an end to the matter because the words had still sliced deeply, for she didn't have the strength to completely refute them as lies yet.

* * * *

The weather was foul on Thursday, and Tabitha was late for class because the bus had been held up by a four-car pileup. The wind snatched at her coat and hair as she struggled the short distance from the bus stop to the college. She left her coat outside the classroom because it was saturated and slipped into her seat beside Alex, trying not to wet him with the water still dripping from her hair and bag.

She heard Amelia snicker at the rear of the classroom. "Wet like fish bait, stinks like fish bait."

Alex turned and glared at her.

Amelia held her nose and waved her hand as if fending off a bad smell.

"Ignore it, Alex," Tabitha whispered.

"Talkative lot today, aren't we? How about a bit of shhh," Kayne said as he dropped his wet briefcase on the desk. He started the lecture immediately.

Twice the lights flickered in the classroom, and thunder repeatedly drowned out Kayne's words, but it was the screech of Tabitha's pager that finally silenced Kayne. Everyone turned to look at her as she pulled it out and read the message.

"Sorry, Kayne, can I leave early? I'm needed for an emergency."

"Sure. Have you got the details for the new assignment?"

"Yes," Tabitha answered, even as she packed her bag.

Alex sat up straight in his seat and grinned at her. "Go, Tabitha," he said loudly as he softly punched her upper arm. "Be careful, though."

She nodded as she hastily finished stuffing her materials

into her backpack. As she left the room, she heard subtle snickers behind her, but for the first time they didn't matter to her. She was on a mission.

By the time her bus rounded the last corner, her pager had gone off four more times. They needed all the crew they could get. The slashing wind and rain had caused upheaval everywhere—flooding, overflowing gutters, leaking roofs and trees down. She grabbed her mother's car keys, yelled, "See you later," and took off out of the door.

The unit was alive with activity. One truck had already gone out, the other was pulled up ready to go and the four-wheel drive with a trailer attached was waiting in the yard. The crew room was crowded and five large men, Isabella and Tabitha juggled around one another to encase themselves in orange overalls, boots, helmets, gloves and rain jackets in the shortest time possible.

As they emerged, PJ issued orders. "Isaac, Isabella, Tabitha and Tim on five forty-four. Here's the job detail. Radio in when you're almost finished. We have another five jobs on the list already. Annie, Phillip and I will head out in the troopy and get a couple of small jobs done. Imogen has come in to manage the radio and ops."

It was only six but an ethereal gloom hung over everything, making it seem much later. The wind shook the truck and rain and hailstones slashed the windscreen as the wipers struggled to keep it clear. The first job was quite close. An elderly lady had water lapping at her front door from where it had overflowed the neighbor's gutter and washed down her driveway. They managed to build a good, strong levy around her veranda by digging trenches and using sandbags they had filled earlier to divert most of the flow down either side of her little unit.

It was icy cold. The wind seemed to slip right through Tabitha's rain jacket and the coarse material of her overalls. Her feet felt like lumps of ice in the stiffness of her boots, which were now covered in red clay mud. Rain dribbled down her face and off the end of her nose, but the crisis had

150

been averted and the lady was tearfully grateful. Despite her physical discomfort, Tabitha felt warm inside. The radio crackled as they drove off and Tabitha wrote down the instructions for the next job.

This time a tree had crashed through the front window of a house, showering the occupants with glass and branches. Water was streaming in through the broken window. The mother had received several cuts to the shoulders and face as she had leaned over her children to protect them and was just leaving in an ambulance when they pulled up. The grandmother had arrived and was trying to calm the three young children about their mother and the tree in the house. Fortunately she took them off in her car to her house before the crew started to work.

Tim and Isabella pulled out chainsaws and fired them up. Tim pointed out to Tabitha where she should work dragging branches away as Isabella cut them. He also warned her again of the danger areas and to wear her safety glasses. The rain continued to pelt down, but after a very short time, Tabitha no longer felt the cold. Perspiration beaded her forehead and fogged up her safety glasses, but she continued to drag branch after branch away from the cutting zone and stacked them in piles in the middle of the lawn. With the sudden ceasing of the chainsaw's roars, the pressure in her ears dissipated. It was silent, except for the weather. Tabitha looked up. Isabella and Tim were both refueling the chainsaws while Isaac was gearing up with chaps over his overalls.

Isabella looked in her direction as she finished the refueling. "It's you and me now, Tabitha. I'm too short to reach the other branches, so Isaac is taking over. When they get down to those two big forks, we need to dig out the large tarpaulin and ropes so we can cover the window, but before we close it completely, we'll try to remove as much tree from inside as we can. Makes it easier for the householder."

They worked on. Every muscle in her body was screaming

for mercy and she had found some she hadn't even known she had. With the last of the tree removed, they erected the tarp. It took all four of them to get it in place as the swirling wind whipped it back and forth. Hail rattled against it and especially strong gusts dragged the ropes around out of reach, but finally it was secure. They added a couple of battens over the top to keep the storm out of the house until the householder could get the damage repaired.

Tabitha had no idea what time it was. There was no moonlight, and as they crossed town, they passed through two whole suburbs that were shrouded in total blackness. They pulled up outside McDonald's and Tim and Isabella scuttled inside to get burgers, fries and drinks. They scarfed them down in the truck. Everyone was starving, and just as they cleaned up the last of the fries, the radio crackled.

New instructions came through and they were underway again. They worked through the night — small jobs and big jobs — clearing fallen trees, sandbagging flooded areas and patching leaking roofs. The last job was replacing tiles on a house roof after a mini tornado had ripped through the street. Tabitha followed Tim as he replaced the tiles down one side of the roof. Her job was to make it waterproof by squeezing silicon in the gaps. Isaac and Isabella worked down the other side of the high hip roof until all that was left was a small hole. They all wore harnesses, but it was still nerve-wracking with the wind ripping at their clothes and snatching at their helmets. Finally a small tarp was secured over the remaining hole and they climbed down off the roof and replaced the ladders and equipment in the truck. It was five a.m. and Tabitha was so weary she struggled to climb into the truck. She was wet through and feeling icy cold now that she had stopped moving. The radio crackled. They were being called back to headquarters — there were four fresh crew members to take over. With the storm easing a little, the jobs would slow to a trickle and they would finally be able to catch up.

Annie, Jesse and Phillip from the other crew had just

finished stripping out of their overalls and hanging them in the dryer. Like Tabitha, their civvies underneath were as wet as the overalls.

"Here, Tabitha, have this. It's a spare one I keep in my locker. At least it will keep the top part of you warm while you drive home," Annie shouted as she threw a sweatshirt across the crew room.

"Thanks, Annie. As long as it's a spare."

"Of course, silly. I'm not that generous, you know." Annie laughed as she pulled on another daggy, oversize sweatshirt over her water-logged clothes.

Tabitha couldn't help smiling. She suspected that Annie was that generous—and more.

"Come on, Pipi, time to go home to a hot shower and a warm bed," Jesse said as he hustled them all out of the crew room just in time for Paul, Squib, David and Toby to enter. Tabitha had only met these four guys briefly before at training, but they grinned a greeting.

"Good job, you guys. Hope you did all the hard ones," Squib joked.

"Oh, we did, Squibby, and most of the easy ones too—just in case you lot of slackers weren't up to it. Enjoy your warm beds, did you?"

The four men guffawed at Jesse's joking swipe at their capabilities.

"Don't you worry, little Jesse James, we can match you any day," Paul crowed as he pulled up his overalls. Then his face smoothed into a serious expression. "So, any problems with the equipment we should know about?" he asked as he did up the studs on his overalls.

"Nope. We serviced the chainsaws and refueled them. The truck is fueled, ready to go. You'll need a couple of tarps or a roll of black plastic though because we used them all."

"Okay. Catch you later, guys," Paul said.

Tabitha still shivered as she crawled into her warm bed. Every muscle ached with strain and tiredness, but she was

153

content. What she and the crew had done tonight amazed her. While she had limited skills, she had been able to contribute, and she remained in awe of the others and how they handled everything from communicating with the client, chainsaws, knots, huge tarps and swaying branches that threatened to swipe your head off as they were buffeted by the wind. Nobody had complained about the conditions — the cold, the wet, the dark or the hard work. In time, she knew she would be just as good as them.

* * * *

When Tabitha stepped eagerly into the classroom on Thursday, it was empty, except for Amelia sitting on her desk. Apprehension crawled along her skin. She felt cornered. Instinctively she went to retreat, then stopped. *No. I'm not going to run away. I will stand my ground. Gosh, I wish I had a chainsaw in my hand right now, I'd cut that damn desk right out from under her.* The mental vision warmed her. She stood just inside the door and stared at her bully.

"So, did you have fun playing the hero then, Tubby Tabby?"

Tabitha looked at this person sitting on her desk — in her space. A smoldering lump of anger flared into fiery flames.

"I don't play at being a hero, Amelia. I go out there and work my butt off to help those who need it. Now, please get off my desk," she snapped.

"Oh, how nice and polite. 'Please get off my desk'." Amelia echoed Tabitha's request and smirked. "Why should I?" she asked.

"Well, I tell you what. Don't. I don't want to sit there anymore, anyway," Tabitha said, quietly, angry at herself because she was trembling as she bent down to pick up her bag.

Amelia made no effort to move. Inside, Tabitha was fighting a turbulent mixture of anger and fear. *Damn this woman.* She turned, took three steps and plonked herself down in the desk one row behind and pulled out her things. Amelia remained sitting on the desk. She pinned Tabitha with a scornful stare. Tabitha lifted her gaze and stared back at her nemesis. She could feel Amelia's gaze drilling into her, willing her to crumble, to look away or show signs of weakness. Tabitha took a deep, deep slow breath and held Amelia's look with a steady sizzling stare of her own. She felt sick with apprehension. Who knew what Amelia would do? She'd been physical before. Their last brawl had left Tabitha with a black eye, a sprained wrist and bruised ribs. But she was determined not to back down. Bugger the fear, she could do this.

The door clattered open and Alex, Leo and Dawn pushed through. Amelia broke her death stare to look at the newcomers, then she flicked Tabitha one more searing look, slid off the desk and walked to the back of the room to take her seat beside Dawn.

Alex leaned close to Tabitha as he slipped in beside her. "What was all that about? You could have cut the air with a knife."

Tabitha sort of hiccupped as she fought down a slightly hysterical chuckle. "Oh, nothing much. Just the worm sort of turned. Just a bit."

"Good on you, Kitty Kat."

"Oh, I'm sure there will be repercussions," she said.

She didn't have to wait long. Less than ten minutes into the tutorial, a ball of something wet and sticky landed in her hair. Tabitha reached up and tried to brush it away, but it wouldn't move. She heard snickers from the back of the room. She ignored them.

Another ball of muck smacked into the back of her head. She ignored it. More snickers. She decided enough was enough. Ignoring Kayne, she suddenly swung around to face them.

She said very quietly and calmly, "For God's sake, children, enough already. Spitballs, really? I would have thought you grew out of that behavior in kindergarten."

Then she turned back to the lecture.

She didn't know if Kayne had heard her or realized what was going on because he just continued with the presentation.

Another missile hit her and one went flying past her and landed with a small splat on the projector. It hissed as the moisture steamed on the hot metal.

The lecturer frowned first at Tabitha, then glared at the three in the back row. "Yes, perhaps they should have. Out, you three. You can come back after the break."

"What? You can't do that," Amelia shouted.

"I can and I have. You're disrupting the tutorial and others want to learn, even if you don't." Kayne's response was quiet but firm.

Alex gave her a small nudge in the leg and Tabitha struggled to control her giggles. Score one for her. The rest of the tutorial was peaceful because the expelled three did not return after the break.

Tabitha fully expected them to be waiting for her between the room and the bus as she slipped out early to go to an extra shift at the vet clinic, but there was no sign of them. Her pager screeched as she arrived at work. She looked at the message on the screen.

Crew wanted at 10:00 hours Saturday for a PR photo shoot. Female members, in particular. Advise if attending.

As she turned the pager off, Tabitha smiled. She didn't know what would be required, but it should be fun. Before she began work, she messaged Louise, Isabella and Annie and they all replied that they would be attending. Louise offered to reply on behalf of all four.

* * * *

Alex pulled her into his embrace as soon as the front door had closed. He kissed her lingeringly, his mouth exploring hers and trailing a hot path from her mouth to her jaw and down her neck. She kissed him back, leaning against him. Her knees felt wobbly and her breath jerked unsteadily. Alex's breath puffed in little hisses as he eased her away from him. She looked up into his eyes, reading signals of passion and desire that matched her own.

Part of her wanted to go further, to discover what drove the warm hum inside, but her more practical side knew she was not ready to take that step. She hoped Alex understood.

He flicked his car keys into the air and caught them. "You know I'm going to wipe the floor with you tonight, Kitty Kat."

She grinned, put her hand on his chest and gently pushed him toward the door. "Don't count your chickens…"

* * * *

The bowling alley was busy, the music loud and the disco lights flashing. They had fun. Tabitha was a lousy bowler so Alex stood behind her, trying to guide her swing. Most often the ball ended up in the gutter, and one time they both almost followed the ball down the lane. They were laughing so much they had to sit to calm down.

It was then that Tabitha saw Jaclyn. She was with her family. Tabitha's amusement died as they looked at each other for a long moment before Tabitha looked away. She wasn't sure what to do. Jaclyn had hurt her, but it wasn't really her fault. Things had gotten pretty nasty.

"Alex, can you get me a drink please, before we start again? I'm going to speak to Jaclyn, she's just over there."

Alex nodded and disappeared. Tabitha made her way slowly to Jaclyn's lane. She waited for her to bowl then beckoned her over. As she approached, Tabitha took her arm and led her to the ladies'.

It was quiet inside. Jaclyn pulled away from her and stood there in silence.

"Jaclyn, I just wanted to say I'm sorry for not speaking to you when you called. I just couldn't."

157

Jaclyn tried to smile. "It's all right, Tabitha. I'm to blame for running out on you after the Facebook stuff. I know it wasn't your fault, but I was just so embarrassed." Her face flushed pink.

"I know, Jaclyn, it was awful."

Tabitha went to turn away, having said what she intended. Jaclyn touched her arm.

"I'm sorry, Tabitha, for letting you down. I have...I have never come across that sort of thing before... Bullying, I mean. After that day at college, I was scared she would start on me. I still like you, Tabitha."

"Well, maybe we can have a coffee in the café one day, Jaclyn," Tabitha said before she turned and walked out of the ladies' and back to the bowling lanes.

Alex was waiting with cold drinks. "So how'd it go?" he asked.

Tabitha shrugged. "Okay. A bit sad really. I liked Jaclyn, I feel better having talked to her, but I am not sure I can be her friend."

"Good. Now let's play. I'm gonna trounce you, Kitty Kat."

By the time they finished, it was neck and neck and Alex admitted it was a draw.

As he dropped her off, he kissed her softly. "Have fun tomorrow."

* * * *

Saturday was bright and sunny. They were all issued new, crisp, bright orange overalls.

"This is so exciting. These photos are going to be used for PR throughout the whole organization. They're encouraging women to get involved too," Louise crowed as she finished doing up her beautifully polished boots.

It looked like chaos outside with a photographer, the PR manager, PJ and about six crew all milling around. The girls stood quietly in a little huddle, trying to stay out of the way as Eddie and his crew set up equipment to allow a stretcher

158

to be lowered from the roof of the shed and for abseiling to be done. It was tricky and only those with considerable experience were allowed to participate.

"Why are you young women hiding away there? Get into a climbing harness, whoever is experienced," the PR manager ordered.

"Just Isabella and Annie for abseiling. Thanks, Margery. They're the only two qualified."

Margery made some notes on her clipboard. "Fine, Peter, but I do want all of your girls in one shot. This shoot is strongly about promoting a female presence in the organization."

Louise and Tabitha watched as Isabella and Annie climbed onto the roof. When they were fully harnessed, they dropped over the guttering and posed three or four times as they lowered themselves slowly down the shed wall.

Margery was hustling the photographer in the direction she wanted. "Fantastic, girls. Now, in the trucks. Who are your truck drivers, Peter?"

"Eddie, Paul and Phillip."

"Okay, one of you boys, hop up. Then we'll fill the rest of the seats with the young ladies."

"Louise and Tabitha, you're up." PJ waved them forward.

It was fun climbing into the truck, posing on the steps and opening up a tray or two in a simulated retrieval of gear. They even posed with chainsaws. Tabitha enjoyed herself immensely, not even feeling shy about her size in front of the camera. This was her thing. She belonged there and she was proud of it.

"Okay, now I want something special. Girls, all of you. Stand here. Arm in arm. Yes, that's right. Now, Gary, I want you to get a photograph from across the road. Now, girls, walk toward the camera, smiling please."

After three attempts, Margery was satisfied that she had the shot she wanted. The 'Chainsaw Chicks', she called it.

When it was finished, the girls changed into their everyday

clothes, still giggling about their sudden rise to fame as the 'Chainsaw Chicks'. Even the guys thought it was a hoot as they gathered at the pub for lunch.

* * * *

After a late SES call-out on Monday night, Tabitha overslept and she was late for college because she missed her bus. Everyone else was already seated in class and Kayne was just about to start the lecture.

"Sorry, Kayne. I missed the bus."

He frowned then turned to the board and began. The few stifled sniggers from the back of the room warned her that Amelia was up to something and that she would be the target of whatever unpleasantness it involved.

At the break, Amelia barely waited until Kayne had left the room before she pounced. "So, Miss Chainsaw Chick, we think we're famous now, do we? Well, I must say orange is just not your color, Tubby, and the camera puts on ten kilos. Not what I would call an alluring publicity shot."

Tabitha turned around to face her abuser. Alex came to stand beside her.

"What the hell are you talking about?" Tabitha asked, confused by her taunts. She had no idea how Amelia would know about the photo shoot the previous the weekend.

"Oh, so you haven't seen yourself then? Probably a good thing, Tubby. Here, for your information," Amelia snarled and thrust the daily paper into her face before she stomped from the room.

Tabitha straightened the crushed pages out and put them in order. And there she was, on page six.

The Chainsaw Chicks of the SES.

It was a fantastic photo with the four of them, arms linked, helmets on their heads and smiles on their faces. In the background was five forty-five and the shed with the unit logo emblazoned on the door.

160

"Wow. I didn't expect it to get in the paper," Tabitha squeaked.

"Hey, you look great, Tabitha," Alex said as he leaned over her shoulder to read the story below.

"You girls look great, and by the way, Tabitha, the camera does not add ten kilos," Leo said.

"Thanks, guys."

"Yes, very good article and great photo, Tabitha. You look like you're enjoying yourself," Kayne said as he walked past.

"I am, Kayne."

As the second half of the lecture started, her three tormentors filed silently back into the room and the rest of the lesson went uninterrupted until Tabitha had to leave to catch her bus for a second extra shift at the clinic. She was about to slip quietly out of the door when her pager began to bleat and vibrate.

"Oh God, here we go again. Miss Chainsaw Chick to the rescue," Amelia sneered.

Tabitha ignored Amelia's sarcasm as she concentrated on her pager screen. As they only wanted a small experienced crew, she wasn't going to attend, but there was no need to let Amelia know that.

"Well, hurry along, Tubby. Go be a hero," Amelia snapped.

Amelia's sarcasm made her cringe, as usual, but even as she stood there in the doorway, pager in hand, Tabitha realized something had changed. It wasn't Amelia. It was her. The burn of acid fear in her stomach wasn't as fierce, and damn that bitch, there were things she could do properly. The crew knew it and so did she and that's what mattered. In a sudden flash of insight, Tabitha realized that Amelia's opinion didn't seem so important or accurate anymore, and was therefore less piercing and painful. She had been allowing this person to hurt her by believing her insults. Angry now, Tabitha turned and looked directly at her tormentor.

161

"I have no need to be a hero, Amelia. All I want to do is help our community, help those less fortunate than I am—those hurting, injured or lost. All I want is to make a positive, caring contribution to a better world, which is more than can be said for you, you measly, foul-mouthed bully. So just shut your bloody gob," she said very quietly and firmly.

As she turned to pass through the door, she glanced at her lecturer. He gave as light, almost imperceptible nod and a ghost of a smile. She didn't respond, still resentful that he hadn't dealt with the situation satisfactorily. As the door closed behind her, she heard the sound of applause and a raucous cheer that could only have come from Alex and Leo.

"Go, Tabitha," Alex yelled.

She was shaking so much she could hardly negotiate the stairs. She'd done it. Answered her back. Told her to shove it. And she, Tabitha, was still alive. The world hadn't caved in. In fact, she felt good, in between the chattering teeth and the shivers that vibrated through her.

* * * *

Grinning to herself about the exhilaration of whizzing down a flying fox at the previous training session, Tabitha pushed through the front doors of the college on Thursday morning. Without warning, her path was blocked. She looked up into Amelia's glowering expression. Petra and Dawn stood silently behind her.

"So the little orange hero's got a big mouth. Getting brave are we, Fishbait?"

Tabitha froze. She glanced around. There wasn't another soul in sight.

Amelia latched onto her arm and made to drag her away from the front door.

"No, you don't," Tabitha yelled, grabbing the door handle with her other hand and pulling away from her bully.

"It's time you were put back in your place, Fishbait."

Tabitha clutched the door handle and pressed her feet hard to the floor. Then cruel fingers were unwinding her grip. Petra and Dawn. She was sliding across the floor.

"Help, help," she yelled.

Her grip on the door loosened. Amelia was dragging her across the floor. Tabitha reached for her phone, but Petra slapped it to the floor.

Now Tabitha swung her fist around and caught Amelia in the shoulder.

"Bitch," Amelia screamed.

She swung Tabitha around. She slumped to the floor, cracking her head on the wall as she landed.

"Owwww," Tabitha moaned and tried to crawl away.

Amelia pounced on her. Tabitha kicked and screamed as Amelia pounded her shoulders and head. Tabitha rolled over and kicked, catching Amelia in the stomach. She howled and fell back. Tabitha crawled away, and, using the wall, she got to her feet. Red caught her eye.

She stepped forward and grabbed the lever. "I'll pull it, Amelia. I'll set the alarm off." Petra and Dawn froze for a moment then scurried back toward the front doors. Tabitha snatched up one of the chairs lining the corridor and held it protectively in front of her. Amelia stalked toward her.

Tabitha stood her ground, tightening her grip on the chair. "No, Amelia. No more. I'm warning you, I'll crack you with this chair if you come closer."

"Fishbait's turned vicious."

"Fishbait's had enough, Amelia. I'm not your punching bag. No more."

Amelia stopped advancing. She cocked her head to one side and stared at Tabitha. "Strange, I didn't think you had it in you, Tubby Tabby." Then she turned and followed Petra and Dawn.

Tabitha lowered the chair and sat in it. Her legs were jelly and a warm trickle of blood ran down her face unnoticed as tears filled her eyes. Then she began to laugh. She had fought back. Big time. Next time would be easier.

Finally feeling calmer, Tabitha made her way to Ms. Forbes' office.

"Tabitha, whatever happened to you?" The principal guided her to a seat. "Cindy, get the first aid box."

"Amelia Eckerton bashed me," Tabitha stated bluntly.

"That young woman is in big trouble. Cindy, fetch Mr. Milburne and find out if Amelia Eckerton is on campus and demand she attend my office now."

Cindy hurried from the room as Ms. Forbes pulled out her camera and took photos of Tabitha's beaten face. Mr. Milburne arrived. He frowned as he examined the damage then helped Ms. Forbes cover the cut to her head and put a blanket around her shoulders. All through this Tabitha sat unmoving, except for the shivers vibrating through her body.

She heard the door crash open and a warm arm encircled her. "Awww, Kitty Kat, my poor Tabitha," Alex murmured. "If only I had been there."

Tabitha looked up. "I fought back, Alex."

He smiled now and kissed her lightly on the cheek. "You did good, Tabitha."

Moments later the paramedics arrived and Mr. Milburne and Ms. Forbes left. As the paramedics dressed her head, loud shouting echoed from the room next door. Tabitha could hear Amelia screaming over Mr. Milburne's reasonable tones. It was hard to interpret what was being said, but when Tabitha heard the word police, Amelia's furious screaming turned to loud sobbing and hysterical pleas for them not to.

In the end the police came and interviewed them both separately, and Tabitha was given the chance to think overnight about whether to press charges or not. In the end she decided not to, but she instantly regretted the decision when Ms. Forbes insisted two days later on a reconciliation session.

Tabitha sighed as she took her seat at the table. Another

bloody waste of time.

Mr. Milburne took his seat as Ms. Forbes doled out tea and biscuits. Tabitha almost laughed. It was so civilized when they were here to discuss a bashing.

Amelia arrived last—alone. She marched into the room and flopped into the vacant chair. "Well, shall we get on with this?" she muttered.

"I would expect you to come with a more positive attitude, Amelia."

"Why?" she asked.

Mr. Milburne leaned forward. "Because, young lady, you are here to make amends for your ugly behavior last week. Expulsion could be on the cards if you don't."

Amelia shrugged.

Resentment at her attitude burned in Tabitha. "Amelia, why do you pick on me? That's all I want to know. Why? I've never done anything to you."

Amelia shrugged and looked down at her lap.

"Well, Amelia, this is your chance to explain," Mr. Milburne prompted.

Again Amelia shrugged.

"Oh, come on, Amelia, you must have something to say after all these years of tormenting me?"

Now Amelia looked directly at Tabitha. "I hate you, that's why. Satisfied?"

Tabitha shook her head. "No, Amelia, I'm not satisfied. Why do you hate me? What have I done to you?"

"Nothing, all right? You've done nothing. I don't know why I pick on you. I just do," Amelia shouted. She stood and paced the room. "I don't know why I'm angry with you, or why I hate you."

"Hate is a very strong word, Amelia. A strong emotion," Mr. Milburne cut in before Tabitha could speak.

"Well, it's how I feel every time I see her. She just riles me up," Amelia shouted. "Like this morning, like right now."

Tabitha wasn't sure what to say. All these years of torment and Amelia couldn't tell her why. She remembered what

Dr. Gause had said. "Is it about the ballet, Amelia? About being a fairy?" she asked.

Amelia stood stock-still for a long moment then turned to face Tabitha. She snorted, a negative sort of sound. "Fairy — you've got to be kidding…"

"But she made you be a tree, Amelia, and your mum let her. I still got to be a fairy because my mum insisted. Are you angry at me…or your mother, Amelia?"

Amelia plonked down in the chair. Tabitha could see the tears filling her eyes. "You don't understand, Tabitha, how it feels. Your mum was always there for you — always."

"It wasn't my fault and yet you've been punishing me all these years."

Amelia looked toward her, her face now red, blotchy and wet with tears. "I was jealous all right. Jealous 'cause your parents cared. You have no idea how much it hurts."

Tabitha winced. "Probably about as much as your bullying hurt me," she said.

Amelia glared up at Tabitha, a sneer curling her mouth out of shape. "Oh, come on, Fishbait, you have no idea."

Tabitha stood. She was trembling. Enough was enough. "I don't think this is working, Mr. Milburne. I don't want to do this anymore."

"But…"

Ms. Forbes began to protest, but Tabitha was already slipping through the door.

Alex leaped out of the chair. "No good?"

Tabitha stepped into his embrace and shuddered against his chest. "No. She's totally unreasonable."

"So are they expelling her?" he asked.

Tabitha pulled back from him and looked up. "Maybe. They're going to counsel her first, but if it is anything like today, it will be a waste of time."

Amelia stormed into the classroom immediately after lunch and headed straight for Tabitha's desk. She paused, leaned down. "If I get thrown out of college, I'm going to get you, Fishbait, just you wait and see."

Tabitha flinched at the sharp, savage tone to the threat. She wanted to run, but instead she glared up at her tormentor. "If you get thrown out, it will be your own bloody fault, and if you try to get me, I will fight back."

"Haha. Them's fighting words, Fishbait. May the best woman win," Amelia sneered and stalked to the back of the classroom.

"I see the counseling has helped," Alex muttered.

Tabitha began to giggle then hastily suppressed it as the tutor walked in.

* * * *

As the days passed, Tabitha was aware of a subtle change in her bully's behavior. While Amelia and her friends sniggered and made nasty comments in undertones, they made no attempt to follow her to the bus or hassle her in the corridors. Alex wasn't totally convinced, but Tabitha began to suspect Amelia wasn't deliberately stalking her like she had done in the past. Despite the changes in Amelia's behavior, Tabitha remained on edge when on campus, but there was no further attempt at a physical attack. She suspected that Ms. Forbes had Amelia under some dire threat of expulsion and police intervention if she didn't back off. Tabitha didn't care what had brought about the change, she just enjoyed the less toxic atmosphere.

Chapter Eight

After the movie, Alex had just ordered burgers when her pager screamed. She looked at the message and felt sick.

Child lost in Terrankin National Park. All crew for immediate dispatch to search area.

Tabitha looked out of the windows. It was a beautiful late winter's day — the sun was shining and a light breeze fluttered through the trees, but that breeze was chilly even now, and would certainly pick up strength and become icy by sunset.

She joined Alex in the queue and tapped him on the shoulder.

"What's up, Tabitha?"

"A call-out — a search for a lost child in the national park. I need to go now. Sorry."

"No probs. Our food is ready. You can eat yours on the way. I'll drop you at the unit."

"Thanks, Alex. You're such a special boyfriend. You never complain when I dash off."

"And so I shouldn't. I think that the SES has been the saving of you. Now eat your burger. It'll give you stamina."

* * * *

Louise, Isabella, Eddie, Tim and Johnno were already getting changed.

"Hurry up, Pipi, if you want to be on the first truck out. There's one spare seat."

She snatched her overalls out of her locker and hauled them on over her jeans, slipping her feet into her boots even as she pulled the overalls up. In the last few weeks, she'd learned a lot about speed dressing.

"You'll need your camel pack filled with water, and help yourself to some snacks out of the store — you'll need them if we're out for long," Louise instructed.

Tabitha hurried to complete her preparations as the others left the crew room, determined not to be left behind. The storeroom was open so she grabbed some barley sugar lollies, some nuts and a couple of bags of small savory biscuits and put them in her side pockets. Louise had filled the spare camel pack, so she grabbed it, hooked it over her shoulder, snatched up her gloves and helmet and hurried out of the door with her laces flapping loosely around her boots.

The others were waiting for her in the big truck. She scrambled up and plopped down beside Isabella. Eddie was driving and Louise was navigating and she barely had her seatbelt on when Eddie turned out onto the road.

"So, what were you doing, Tabitha, on this beautiful Saturday afternoon?" Tim asked, his tone full of mock sacrifice and misery.

"Just getting burgers after a movie with my boyfriend."

"What did you see?" Eddie asked without looking around.

"Oh, that new sci-fi one," Tabitha replied.

"Any good?" Johnno asked from beside her.

"I enjoyed it," Tabitha said.

"So did I," Louise piped up from the front. "I saw it last week with my boyfriend."

For the rest of the journey they swapped movie and sob stories about what they had given up to be there. Not that anyone would be anywhere else, despite the sacrifice.

As they entered the park, they fell silent. The seriousness of this trip was suddenly large and imposing. The huge trees on either side of the road were thick and tall, their canopy shaded the ground below in gloomy semidarkness.

169

Ahead they could see hills and more thick bush, only broken at intervals by sharp, steep escarpments that looked like bleeding gashes in the landscape.

The campground was crawling with emergency personnel, park rangers, police and the SES dog squad that came out for special jobs such as searches. They waited in the truck while Eddie went to get instructions.

He came back with a map and a photo of the child. "Okay, guys, we've been allocated some of the roughest terrain. Isabella, you're on radio, Johnno will carry climbing gear and, Tabitha, you're group first-aider. Louise, you're navigator. Tim, you'll mark the outer edge of the grid. They don't know exactly how long he's been missing, but he was here for breakfast at seven. Apparently he was left in the care of his nineteen-year-old aunt while the parents went on a strenuous hike down to the waterfall. The aunt and kid, who is four, had a falling out and the kid took off. Okay, let's go. Oh, by the way, the kid's name is Sebastian."

They moved at a steady pace through the bush. The first aid kit was heavy on Tabitha's shoulders, but not unbearably so. The sun was deceptively warm but hardly counteracted the chilly breeze blowing in their faces. It was almost dark in the heavily shaded spots among the thickest of the trees, and in places the thick vegetation was nearly impassable and the ground rough and uneven. Branches grabbed and snatched at them as they passed. Several times Tabitha was very thankful she had her gloves and safety glasses on as prickly branches whipped at her hands and face.

When they reached their designated area, Louise marked the corner of the grid with a small piece of orange tape then, spaced about two meters apart, they set out through the scrubland. It was rough going in places as they worked their way up the side of their grid, searching every bush, rock and cranny and periodically calling out. When they reached the coordinates of the end of their search grid, they turned and spread out from the markers Tim had placed on the far side of their line. In a slow-moving line, they covered the next strip. Tabitha found it sort of lonely as they worked in relative silence listening for any noise a child might make in between bellowing his name. Up and down they worked, but at the end of the gridded area, they hadn't found any sign of the child or his passage through the area.

They trudged back to the campground for a short break and some food before they would be allocated their next grid. There were three more SES trucks at the campsite, including one of theirs. Paul, PJ, Annie, Isaac and Jesse had already been allocated a grid.

Tabitha was eager to get going again, but Eddie just chuckled.

"Plenty of time to cool your heels on a search, Tabitha. A lot of hurry up and wait. We'll be out again shortly, though, because they need to get as much done before dark as they can. Poor little mite might not survive a night in the cold," Eddie said.

Tabitha sat back and tried to be patient. She drank the hot chocolate Isabella gave her, glad of its warmth. The sun had already dipped to the horizon and was nothing more than a suffused golden glow through the trees. It was getting much colder.

Isabella leaned in and whispered in her ear, "Look over there. That's the parents and the aunt. The boy's father is furious. I assume she's his sister. Both the women are in a bad way, emotionally."

Tabitha looked up in the direction Isabella had discreetly indicated.

Her world fell with a thud, all the way into her boots. Amelia hunched in front of a tall, bearded man. He was yelling at her. She was crying and flinching as he waved his hands around in front of her face. A blonde woman stood behind him, sobbing hysterically.

Tabitha felt sick as she leaned into Isabella. "My God, I know the aunt—that's the girl who bullies me all the time. The one who drove me to suicide. Oh my God..." she exclaimed in a very hushed whisper.

"Well, looks like she's getting some of her own back. You can see where she gets her aggressive nature from," Isabella said.

"Poor Amelia. I know she's a bitch, but I wouldn't wish this on anyone—even my worst enemy, which she is," Tabitha breathed into Isabella's ear.

"No, you're right, it's a horrible thing to happen to anyone, especially the little bloke," Isabella whispered back.

Tabitha sat back and watched as Amelia was harried and berated by her older brother. She knew how it felt, and she was torn between sympathy for her and triumph that her nemesis was suffering a dose of what she dished out constantly.

"Okay, guys, next grid. It will be heavy going. Get a torch and a set of batteries from the truck. Take care out there. We don't want any injuries," Eddie ordered.

It wasn't quite dark as they trudged up the narrow track. Tabitha took one last look at her nemesis. Amelia was now standing alone by a large gum, watching them leave. Their gazes locked for a brief moment, sparking a slight flash of apprehension through Tabitha, but it was gone before she could really acknowledge it. She was strong—she was wearing orange and Amelia couldn't hurt her. Neither acknowledged the other and Tabitha felt relief when she was out of Amelia's sight.

It was a long uphill haul and back again. It was going to be a long night. The stars were twinkling above in a dark velvety sky. It was icy cold and Tabitha's nose was a frozen lump on her numb face and her fingers were stiff inside the leather gloves. It was a lonely task as they searched the bush, meters apart, but as they turned for the next sweep, they had to bunch together to allow for a deep rocky ravine on the left. They halted and Tabitha and Eddie crouched on the edge of the drop and shone their torches down into the pitch-black hollow. As the arc of white light swept the ravine, several pairs of shining eyes reflected silver then flitted, jumped and disappeared.

"Can you see anything?" Tim asked.

"Nope," Eddie yelled. "Just some roos."

Tabitha scanned the gully one more time just to be sure. As the torchlight highlighted every nook and cranny of the ravine walls, she thought she saw something just on the edge of her arc of light. "Eddie, bring your torch over here."

He joined her and the two beams illuminated the side of the ravine.

"There. Do you see it? Right there on that ledge." Tabitha pointed as she tried to keep her torch steady.

"Yeah, I see it. Good spotting, Tabitha. We have something," Eddie shouted as he patted her on the back.

A splash of blue against the red ocher rock. It didn't move and didn't respond when they called. Maybe it wasn't little Sebastian, but he had been wearing a blue puff vest when last seen at the campsite.

"We're going down. Isabella, you're the lightest. Johnno and Tim, set up on those two gums. They're sturdy enough," Eddie ordered. "Tabitha, help Isabella get kitted up, and make sure you double the harness ends back through those buckles, okay?"

Tabitha nodded. She felt scared at the responsibility, but excited that she had found a clue. Fifteen minutes later, Isabella was abseiling down the cliff. It was perilous. The rock wall was loose and gravelly, making solid footholds difficult. But Isabella was a seasoned abseiler and knew how to place her feet to get maximum support. Tabitha helped Tim and Johnno control the lines while Eddie peered over the edge to track Isabella's progress. Tension surrounded them as they waited for Isabella to reach her target.

"It's the boy," she cried as she scrambled onto the narrow sloping ledge.

"How's his condition?" Eddie asked.

They waited. Tabitha barely breathed as they all stood frozen in anticipation and apprehension.

"He's alive. Pulse is weak. I think his leg is broken, and

he's been spiked by a tree branch in the top of his arm. It's still oozing blood and he has some cuts and bruises on his legs and arms."

"Okay, first aid pack on its way down. Watch out below," Eddie yelled as he let the first aid kit slowly slide down to Isabella.

Johnno was already radioing back to base about their find, his condition and the coordinates. There was no way a vehicle could get in because of the rough ground or a chopper because of the dense bush and towering trees. They would have to carry him out.

"Okay, guys, we wait. The others are on their way. They have a tripod, a stretcher and a paramedic with them. We'll send down two more and the stretcher to get him up. Then the paramedic will take over his care, and we'll all take turns to carry him back to the campsite because that's the nearest place a vehicle can get in. He's only a little guy, so it shouldn't be too heavy. Rest up, guys," Eddie instructed as he settled himself on a flat boulder by the ravine.

Tabitha took one more look over the edge. Isabella waved. Tabitha could see the boy easily now because he was wrapped in a silver thermo blanket. All they could do was wait. The temperature plunged and Tabitha shivered. At least when they were searching, the movement had kept her warm. Now that they were stationary, the quietness of the bush surrounded them with just an occasional bird whistle or a scrabbling of an animal in the darkness to break the quiet. The wind whispered in the leaves. Nobody talked much and Eddie and Johnno napped against the trunk of a nearby tree in between taking turns to observe Isabella and the child. Louise sat next to her.

"So, Tabitha, did you ever see yourself doing this?" she asked.

"Not really, but then, I didn't see myself abseiling either."

Louise tucked her hands in her pockets to ward off the cold. "How bad is the bullying with that girl back there?"

"Pretty bad, but Annie taught me about fogging and how

to appear nonchalant when you're not. I've been practicing at home."

"Does it actually work?" Louise asked.

Tabitha moved slightly to ease the numbness in her backside. "Well, sort of. It did shut her up the other day. Thank goodness there have been no more physical attacks. That really scared me."

"So what about now? Do you think she'll change toward you?" Louise asked.

Tabitha shrugged. "She probably won't, but I've changed...I feel stronger inside, knowing I can do things... Volunteering was the best thing I've ever done."

Louise laid her arm around Tabitha's shoulders. "Never forget you have mates, Tabitha—we like you, and you should like yourself—a lot."

"I know, Louise, and I'm beginning to like me. Well, at least I don't think I'm such a failure anymore."

"Excellent, that's a start. You're a good person, Tabitha— you have to believe that."

Tabitha nodded but didn't reply. She knew she had a ways to go to like the person she was, but now she believed it would happen. They sat in companionable silence on the boulder under the cold night sky studded with millions of stars.

It seemed like forever, but finally the other crew arrived and, working like a well-oiled machine, they erected the tripod with ropes, pulleys and carabiners, all checked and in place. Paul and Eddie climbed delicately down the ravine wall. Tabitha watched in fascination. One day she would do this.

At last the stretcher swung up out of the ravine and was gently set onto flat ground. The paramedic immediately examined the now barely conscious Sebastian. He announced that Isabella's first aid was more than satisfactory, added a drip, oxygen and some pain medication.

Eddie issued brisk instructions. "Okay, guys. Tabitha, Isaac, Johnno and I will take first turn. Then Paul, PJ, Louise and Annie. Let's move out."

The stretcher wasn't heavy, but it was challenging transporting the injured child through the thick bush, over loose rocks and dark indentations in the ground.

It was icy-cold, but Tabitha was sweating as she took her second turn at carrying the stretcher. Her legs were nothing more than numb, pumping protrusions carrying her through the bush when at last she saw the lights of the campground ahead. The parents waited by the bottom of the trail. Amelia stood a bit behind them with her parents, who had obviously arrived on the scene to help while Tabitha and the crew were out searching. A storm of weeping had ravaged Amelia's face and she was still crying. Farther back, several reporters tried to take photos. The police held them at bay as the crew, with the stretcher, pushed past, ignoring the cameras and microphones shoved in their faces. With hardly a pause, they loaded the child, stretcher and all, into the ambulance. His mother got in with him and it roared away, lights flashing and siren screaming.

The boy's father and Amelia were already being bundled past the press into a waiting police car. For a moment, Amelia hesitated by the open car door. She looked straight at Tabitha and gave the slightest of nods. Tabitha nodded back before she quickly turned away. She was not ready to make peace with Amelia Eckerton just yet, but she was pleased that the child was safe and she had helped. It also pleased her that Amelia had acknowledged that in some slight way.

* * * *

Tuesday morning Tabitha met Amelia at the classroom door. Her bully looked tired and haggard. "How's your nephew?"

"Recovering, thank you," Amelia replied.

Tabitha opened the door and stood back. "After you," she said.

Amelia didn't respond, just walked through the door and made her way to the back of the room.

At the end of the morning tutorial, they were both summoned to another counseling session. Tabitha didn't want to go. She hung back with Alex until Amelia was long gone, then she dawdled upstairs to the meeting room.

The three of them were waiting when she entered the room, and she felt uncomfortable and defensive as the conversation stopped suddenly.

"Sorry I'm late," she said, sliding into the one spare chair.

"Amelia arranged this meeting last Friday, but she has just explained what happened over the weekend," Ms. Forbes said quietly.

Tabitha nodded. "What happened at the weekend does not change anything."

Amelia leaned forward. "No, Tabitha, it doesn't change anything between you and me because I had already faced up to my demons. You were right, you know. I have been punishing you for my parents' failures. I see it even more after the weekend. They've disowned me. Darren was even meaner to me than usual and Roz, Sebastian's mother, won't speak to me at all—like I did it on purpose."

"And this is to do with me, how?" Tabitha asked.

Amelia shook her head. "I was jealous of you—I wanted what you had, loving parents. I know it was pathetic, but I was too scared to take it out on them. You were an easy target for my anger."

"You know it wasn't fair."

Amelia nodded. "I know now. I'm sorry, but I can't take it back."

Tabitha wavered between wanting to scream at her bully and being sick. After all this time, two simple words—'I'm sorry'—were expected to wipe out all the misery. Tabitha knew it wouldn't, couldn't, and that the scars on her soul would remain forever. Amelia would never understand the damage she had done and Tabitha knew she could never explain it to her, and it didn't matter anyway for it didn't change anything. All she could do was accept the apology and move on with a hard lesson learned.

"No, you can't take back all the pain you caused, Amelia, but if this is an end to it, I'll accept your apology so we can both move on."

"Thank you, Tabitha, for being so generous, and if it's any consolation to you, it's my turn now — my family are angry with me and not about to let me forget my mistake. Darren keeps on and on about it, telling me I'm an idiot and useless. I begged Mum to tell him to stop, but she just shrugged and said he's very upset and I'll have to live with it until he calms down."

Tabitha frowned. "It's no consolation to me, Amelia, but I do know how it feels to be called names."

"No, it's not very nice," she replied, her face flushing a deep red.

Tabitha stood to leave. Ms. Forbes was smiling and Tabitha felt happy for her. Today she hadn't failed.

"So you're smiling. Don't tell me you've had a breakthrough?" Alex asked as soon as the door closed behind her.

Tabitha hugged him. "Yep, I think it's sorted."

* * * *

Amelia ignored Tabitha through the afternoon class and Petra and Dawn followed her lead, but Tabitha got a little jumpy when she realized Amelia was following her to the bus. Despite the positive outcome of the counseling session, Amelia hadn't actually promised to stop her behavior. Tabitha had no intention of being browbeaten anymore.

"Tabitha, wait up," Amelia called.

Tabitha hesitated and glanced over her shoulder, but kept moving. She had no desire to talk to Amelia Eckerton.

"Please wait. I have something for you," Amelia shouted.

Tabitha stopped and turned then. "I thought we settled everything this morning, Amelia. No more bullying, and I would prefer you just stay out of my way."

Amelia held out a box, all wrapped in pink paper and ribbon. "I wasn't going to be mean, I just wanted to give you this—for you and the crew, to say thanks for saving Sebastian."

"Oh. I see. No thanks are needed, but the crew will appreciate them," Tabitha replied as she glanced over Amelia's shoulder, looking for the bus. She didn't want to be standing here with her tormentor.

"Tabitha, I just want to say I thought you were great— you and everyone."

"I will pass your thanks on to everyone," Tabitha responded politely as she took the big box of chocolates Amelia held out.

Without another word, Tabitha turned to get on the bus as it squeaked to a halt.

Her heart was beating an erratic tattoo as she took her seat. As the bus pulled away, she could see Amelia standing at the bus stop all alone. She breathed in a deep, slow breath. Amelia no longer terrified her.

* * * *

That night she opened up Facebook for the first time since her suicide attempt. There was very little on her newsfeed, but several friend requests had come through—Isabella, Annie, Louise and Jesse. She confirmed them all. Then she posted some photos of herself on her profile—one abseiling, another using a chainsaw, one on the truck the night of her very first call-out and, of course, the 'Chainsaw Chicks'. She changed her profile pic to one of her and Alex out riding and clicked 'in a relationship'.

She sat back and looked at what she'd done. This profile represented who she now was. It felt like she'd made a new start. A new, better, stronger Tabitha had risen out of the pain and humiliation of the old one.

Moments later, the phone rang. "So you're back on

Facebook?" Alex asked.

"Yes, I thought I would give it a go. The other profile is gone, thank God. So have you looked at my real profile yet?"

"Yup. Best bit—us together and 'in a relationship'," he said.

She laughed. "I was a bit worried about putting it up there, but you did say the other day you were my boyfriend," she said.

"Yup, I did and I meant it. I must admit, you're a changed woman since joining the SES, and you know what, I like it—a hell of a lot."

Her face began to burn. "Thank you," she croaked.

"So we on for Friday night? It's my mate's twenty-first."

"Yes," she said with a sudden rush of nervousness. "I haven't met any of your mates before."

"They won't bite, Tabitha. Besides, I think it's time I introduced you to the crowd."

* * * *

She fretted about this social engagement. What if she didn't fit in? What should she wear? Tabitha was very aware that most of Alex's mates were, like him, several years older than her, and it worried her that they might find her immature. On Friday morning she changed her outfit for the third time then flopped in front of her laptop. She studied the picture of her abseiling and smiled— these strangers couldn't be any more scary than her first rappel down the shopping center wall. And because they were Alex's friends, she doubted any would taunt her like Amelia, especially with Alex by her side—well, at least some of the time. She decided in that moment she was going to enjoy herself.

The music was loud and people were wandering into the brightly lit house. As they got out of the car Alex grabbed her arm and held out a coin.

"Toss you for who drives home," he said, grinning.

She grinned back. "Fine. I want heads not to drive," she said.

"Okay, so if heads comes up I drive, you drink."

She nodded, almost offering right then and there to be the designated driver. She wasn't that fussed about alcohol, but she knew Alex liked to have a couple of beers. She let him toss the coin, knowing it was a sign of the equality in their relationship and she liked it that way.

"Oooops, Kitty Kat, it's tails. Do you mind very much?" Alex asked as he scooped the coin off the ground.

She grinned. "Terribly, Alex."

"Well, we can both not drink, or get a cab," he said, his voice soft and apologetic.

She slapped his arm softly. "Don't be silly, Alex. Of course I don't mind."

He grinned, took her arm and they headed to the party.

There was no chance to hide or even be nervous, for Alex dragged her around introducing her to everyone he knew, and everyone made her welcome.

As they approached another group of his friends, a short guy with blond curly hair grabbed Alex's shoulder. "Oh by the way, Alex, Jim's over there." He waved in the direction of a very tall red-haired man in the corner. "His girlfriend's in the SES too, so if Tabitha gets lonely she can talk to Louise."

The name Louise shimmied across her skin. Surely not her Louise? Alex steered her through the dancing crowd in the center of the room.

"Hi, mate, long time between drinks."

Jim nodded. "Life's not like uni, mate—all work, work, work these days. I've joined a practice down south. The head vet's a bit of a tyrant."

"Yeah, a bit of a bugger."

"Well, you should come back and finish the course. Get your qualifications so we can start our own practice like we planned."

181

"Jim, honey, here's your drink."

Tabitha grinned. "Hi, Louise, fancy meeting you here," she said.

"Tabitha," Louise squealed and grabbed her tightly. "Jim, this is Tabitha from SES."

"Hi, Tabitha, nice to meet you, and, Louise, honeybun, this is my uni mate, Alex."

Louise shook hands with Alex then looked at Tabitha. "Well, aren't you a dark horse? If I'd known, we could have gone on a double date."

Tabitha laughed. "It's only new, and with everything that's happened..."

Louise grinned. "But we will, won't we, fellas?" she asked the two men.

They both nodded obediently before heading for the bar.

Louise grabbed her arm. "Wow, this is fantastic, that you're going out with Alex. Jim was so disappointed when Alex dropped out of uni."

Tabitha looked toward Alex. He and Jim had their heads close together, deep in conversation. She wondered what they were discussing.

"Well, maybe he'll go back, he's really into the racehorses at the moment."

"Would you mind? It's a lot of study time," Louise asked as she glanced over her shoulder at the men.

Tabitha shrugged. "No, I wouldn't mind. I have my own course to finish, and besides I'm a bit too young to get locked into anything serious."

Louise laughed. "And of course you've got the SES to keep you occupied."

"I certainly have."

* * * *

The next couple of weeks at college seemed quiet. Amelia came and went. Most of the time she looked pale and drawn. She said little in class and nothing to Tabitha. Tabitha was

182

glad the abuse had stopped, but she still couldn't shake the feeling that it wasn't quite over. The uneasy, unwritten truce between her and her nemesis ebbed and flowed for the remainder of the term. When she fretted about it, Alex told her to let it go, it was over. She tried to, but somehow a shadow still hung over her. It was like there was something still to be said or done.

At the end of the last lecture, Tabitha found she had passed with excellent results. Alex was stoked too, for not only had he also passed, but he'd been offered a place back at the School of Animal and Veterinary Sciences based on his marks. Tabitha was ecstatic for him.

Alex had to hurry because he had a course to complete at the stables, so Tabitha was left standing alone at the bus stop. She saw Amelia coming, but chose to ignore her. The girl could no longer hurt her, or scare her.

"Tabitha, I wanted to say something before you left."

Tabitha looked at Amelia, but remained silent, wondering just what Amelia felt she needed to say. "I just wanted to say thank you, again, for saving my nephew, especially after the way I treated you. I'm sorry."

"Really?" Tabitha asked, an edge of sarcasm in her tone.

"Yes. I didn't really mean for you to kill yourself – really, I didn't. I don't want us to be enemies anymore."

"Amelia, I was never your enemy – just your victim."

The other girl hung her head. "I don't know why I was so nasty to you. You're a good person, Tabitha. I'm sorry for the way I treated you."

"Yes, Amelia, I am a good person, and now that I actually believe in myself you can't hurt me anymore, but I do appreciate your apology." She turned on the last word and boarded the bus that had just arrived.

For the first time she felt free – really free. She didn't even bother to look back as the bus drove off. There was no need. Amelia no longer mattered.

She sat back in the bus, contented. It had been a big year and she felt so much older today than she had on the first day of college. What more could she ask? She had conquered her nemesis, found a boyfriend, made new friends and taken up a vocation that would challenge her for a long time to come.

Life was suddenly very good and she was glad to be alive.

THE ABRASAXON'S DAUGHTER
THE DANGEROUS QUEST BRINGS MORE THAN SHE EVER EXPECTED

The Scorpion's Heart

DIONIE MCNAIR

The Scorpion's Heart

Excerpt

Chapter One

Brianna paused at the top of the steep track scarcely long enough to catch her breath and check that the anjoa fruit had survived her hurried climb intact. A sense of pride flashed through her as she lifted the concealing cloth. The two oval fruit were the biggest and most beautiful specimens she had ever seen. The green skin of both was smooth and shiny—not a blemish in sight. They would be her offering for the Luna Goddess' table in the temple tomorrow night.

With reverent care, Brianna covered them again, and clutching the wicker basket close to her chest, she hurried through the orchard.

A sharp slice of stinging pain cut across her ankle. Her foot jerked out from under her and she toppled forward, the basket flying out of her grip. Her face slammed into the dirt. The air in her lungs rushed out with the impact.

"Oww," she croaked as she lifted her head and gasped for air.

Her basket rested on its side only inches in front of her, but both of her anjoa fruit had rolled away. "No," she cried and pushed herself to her knees as the biggest wobbled across the last inches of grass and slammed into the rock cairn marking the border of the orchard. It split open, the sweet red flesh torn into ragged chunks, juice and black seeds splattering the grass in a wide circle.

"My offering, oh my beautiful offering," Brianna howled as tears blurred her vision.

Somebody snickered. She turned toward the sound. Conal stood legs apart, arms crossed. At his feet lay the second anjoa fruit, still intact. Behind him waited the four boys who made up his bevy — the rich kids, Tobin, Kedem, Fabron and Rayan.

"Bit clumsy, Brianna," Conal said, a smirk twisting his mouth.

She climbed to her feet. One ankle was entangled in a grubby piece of rope. Unease stabbed through her.

"Well, I still have one," she replied, stepping forward to retrieve the fruit.

Conal rested his foot on it, very gently. "No you don't."

"Yes I do, Conal. Give it to me."

"Why should I?"

"Because it's mine. I brought them all the way from the forest," Brianna replied.

Conal scowled in the direction of the smashed fruit. "But you didn't take care of your gift for the Luna Godess, did you?"

"I would have, if you hadn't tripped me," she shouted, flinging the rope in his direction.

"Ha ha, don't blame me for your big clumsy peasant feet."

Rage burned a fiery path through her veins, melting her self-control into stinging sparks inside her gut. She glared at Conal. "Give it back," she said.

"I don't think so, peasant. The boys and I will take the

186

surviving anjoa to the temple. Clearly you can't be trusted with the task," Conal scoffed.

A searing pain wrenched inside her, as if something had broken. She winced but kept her gaze on Conal, trying desperately to hold down the tight pressure threatening to overcome her. "Give it back," she bit out between clenched teeth. Something was wrong. A writhing, spiny ball of wrath twisted her stomach and she could hardly breathe.

Conal slowly bent down and scooped up the anjoa fruit. He cradled it in his arms and stared at her. "You appear mighty mad and all red in the face, Brianna. But you can't make me give it back."

His taunt stoked her rage. Brianna gasped at the painful implosion as her gut twisted, her lungs compacted and her hands sizzled and flexed with lives of their own. She trembled in a desperate attempt to hold the seething fury inside, but it was too big for her, rampaging with uncontrolled violence. Oh raving hojaks, what was happening to her? The power built until without warning it spurted from her clenched fists in a shimmering, pulsing stream that sprayed directly at the jeering boy.

The translucent force hit Conal in the chest, lifted him off the ground, threw him backward then dumped him on his knees in the dust. The anjoa fruit jumped out of his grip and floated in the air, twisting and turning several times before it landed with a soft plop by Brianna's shoes.

The four boys gaped as Conal very cautiously climbed to his feet and dusted himself off. The energy drained out of Brianna as she stared aghast at Conal. Oh moonbeams, had she done that?

"Run. Everyone run. Brianna's bedeviled by a Tyban. Run for your lives," Conal yelled.

The five boys fled, their screams piercing the air in terror-stricken gashes.

Brianna stood frozen, uncertainty swept over her in undulating waves and she swallowed hard on the surge of nausea that swirled in her stomach. She sagged onto a tree stump and covered her face with her hands. Oh fiery moonlight, moonbeams and luna darkness. What was wrong with her? Bedeviled? Oh dear Luna Goddess, no. Tremors raged through her. Her teeth clattered and she was so cold. The anjoa fruit she had fought to recover sat forgotten at her feet as she hunched protectively in on herself.

A light touch on her shoulder was enough to manifest her terror. She screeched and spun around, ready to defend herself.

"Mam," she cried. "Thank the moons."

"Come away into the house, daughter. There has been enough spectacle today to set tongues wagging from here to Okiyarra."

"I'm not bedeviled, am I, Mam? Is it a Tyban?"

Her mother's grip on her shoulders, urging her toward the house, was forceful.

"No, Brianna, it's not a Tyban."

"But something happened… I felled Conal. I was so angry and it just happened."

"I know."

"But how…? What?" Brianna wailed.

Her mother guided her through the doorway and slammed the door shut. "I know, Brianna, because I've been expecting it."

Brianna pushed away from her mother and looked up into her eyes. What she saw reflected there ballooned her uneasiness into real terror. "Expecting what?"

"Sit, Brianna, and I will explain."

About the Author

Dionie McNair

Dionie was a closet writer for several years before she got brave enough to share her work with anyone, until she joined Eyre Writers Inc, a creative writing group in the seaside town of Port Lincoln and really began to improve.

Her first book was a 100,000 words family saga novel but after studying children's literature at university she embarked on a new direction—writing a young adult fantasy novel.

After being made redundant from the job she loved in 2011 she became a carer for her frail, vision-impaired mother and turned to fulfilling her dream of becoming a writer.

When Dionie is not writing she enjoys spending time with family and friends, especially her mother and three wonderful adult children and adorable grandchildren. She also enjoys egg decorating and carving, reading of course, painting, gardening and cooking.

Dionie currently lives in the beautiful 'city of churches', Adelaide South Australia.

Dionie McNair loves to hear from readers. You can find contact information, website details and an author profile page at https://www.finch-books.com/